"Belle—"

"Don't touch me," she said in a strained voice.

"Belle!" Jake was desperate now. "I didn't know. I didn't know what to think."

"You didn't believe me," she said, her eyes as clear and cold as an arctic lake. "Do you think this makes a difference? Do you honestly think because my mother has absolved me of all blame that I'll forgive you for what you've done? Grow up, Jake. I don't need your absolution. I don't need anything anymore."

Passion™

in

Harlequin Presents®

Looking for sophisticated stories that **sizzle**?
Wanting a read that has a little extra **spice**?

Pick up a Presents *Passion*™ novel—
where **seduction** is *guaranteed!*

Available only from Harlequin Presents®

Anne Mather

SINFUL TRUTHS

Passion™

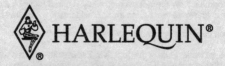

HARLEQUIN®

TORONTO • NEW YORK • LONDON
AMSTERDAM • PARIS • SYDNEY • HAMBURG
STOCKHOLM • ATHENS • TOKYO • MILAN • MADRID
PRAGUE • WARSAW • BUDAPEST • AUCKLAND

ISBN 0-373-12344-2

SINFUL TRUTHS

First North American Publication 2003.

Copyright © 2003 by Anne Mather.

This edition published by arrangement with Harlequin Books S.A.

® and TM are trademarks of the publisher. Trademarks indicated with
® are registered in the United States Patent and Trademark Office, the
Canadian Trade Marks Office and in other countries.

Visit us at www.eHarlequin.com

Printed in U.S.A.

CHAPTER ONE

THE apartment was in one of the more expensive parts of the city. Not a high-rise, despite the many luxury apartments that were available in that kind of real estate. No, the apartment Isobel had chosen was on the upper floor of a converted Victorian townhouse, and what it lacked in modern amenities it more than made up for in style and elegance.

It didn't surprise Jake that she had preferred the older building. Isobel came from old money, and, however straitened her circumstances, she'd rather freeze in rooms that had never been intended to be warmed by central heating than live in comfort in contemporary uniformity.

Not that it hadn't been expensive. Jake knew exactly how expensive it had been. He should do, he reflected ironically. He'd bought it for her when they separated, and he'd held the lease on it ever since.

Jake had to park his car on the adjoining street and walk the couple of hundred yards to Eaton Crescent. It was raining, typical May weather, and he scowled as the downpour soaked the shoulders of his leather jacket. Another jacket bites the dust, he thought resignedly, wondering when he'd got used to discarding clothes like unwanted parking tickets. He should have used an umbrella. There was a golfing one in the boot of his car, put there by a grateful salesman when he'd bought the expensive vehicle. Needless to say, it had never been used.

There was a panel beside the door with the names of the various occupants of the apartments beside individual bells. It was supposed to be for security purposes, but Jake knew

that persistent callers simply rang all the bells until someone was foolish enough to let them in. There was no in-
tercom, and although at the time he'd bought it he'd ex-
pressed his doubts to Isobel, she had been indifferent to his
concerns.

'Don't pretend you care what happens to us,' she'd declared coldly, on their way back to the estate agent's office,
and he'd refused to take the bait.

Now, pushing back the thoughts of that ugliness, Jake
pressed Isobel's bell and waited for the door to unlatch.
She knew he was coming so she could hardly pretend to
be out.

He didn't have to wait long. Almost immediately the
catch was released and he pushed open the door into the
hall.

Despite its rather gloomy interior, the hall smelled pleasantly of pot-pourri and furniture polish. A cleaning service
kept the public halls and stairways in excellent repair, and
the immediate impression was of warmth and gentility.

The door closed automatically behind him, and after
brushing a careless hand over his wet hair Jake mounted
the carpeted stairs two at a time. He was breathing a little
heavily when he reached the second landing, and he reminded himself that he hadn't been to the gym in a while.
Sitting in front of a computer might be easier than cutting
rocks, so to speak, but it was a hell of a lot less healthy.

Isobel's door wasn't open. He'd thought it might have
been as she'd obviously let him in, but it wasn't. Restrain-
ing the impulse to try the handle, he lifted his hand and
knocked, waiting a little impatiently for her to answer.

But Isobel didn't answer the door. Emily did. And she
stood glaring at him with all the rage and resentment he'd
used to expect from her mother.

'What do you want?'

Her question took him by surprise. He'd felt sure Isobel

would have discussed his visit with her. But clearly she hadn't, and he was left having to explain to a precocious ten-year-old that her mother was expecting him.

'Well, she's not here,' Emily declared with evident satisfaction. 'So you'll just have to come back some other time.'

Jake blinked. 'You're not serious,' he said, recalling the trouble he'd had keeping this appointment in the first place. Not to mention the bitch of having to park in the next street and walk half a mile in the pouring rain.

'Yeah, I am, actually,' the girl responded smugly. She was obviously enjoying his frustration. She made as if to close the door again. 'I'll be sure and tell her you called—'

'Wait!' Before she could slam the door in his face, Jake wedged his foot against the jamb. He winced as the heavy wood thudded against his boot, but he held firm, and Emily was eventually forced to admit defeat.

'Mummy's not going to like this, you know,' she exclaimed, tossing back her plait of dark brown hair. 'You can't tell me what to do.'

'I can and I will,' retorted Jake grimly. 'Now, why don't you stop behaving like a brat and tell your mother I'm waiting?'

'I've told you, she's not here,' declared Emily, her voice wobbling a little now. 'Who do you think you are, trying to force your way in here, frightening me?'

Jake had thought it would take rather more than his not unfamiliar presence to frighten Isobel's daughter, but perhaps he was wrong. In any event, he was suddenly reminded that despite the fact that she was tall for her age— and insolent, as he knew to his cost—she was still a child, and he regretted losing his temper with her.

So all he said was, 'I'm your mother's husband. Now, where is she? She knew I was coming. Why the—why isn't she here?'

Emily pursed her lips. 'She's at Granny's,' she admitted after a minute. 'I don't know how long she's going to be.'

'At your grandmother's?' Jake felt his temper simmering again, and determinedly tamped it down. But he should have known that Lady Hannah would have some hand in this. She had never liked him, never approved of her daughter having anything to do with him. Never accepted that without his help she wouldn't still own that mouldering pile she called the family seat.

Now he took a deep breath. 'You don't mean she's in Yorkshire, do you?'

'No.' Emily pouted. 'She's at a Granny's flat.'

'Right.' At least that wasn't a couple of hundred miles away. 'What's she doing there?' he asked, proud that no evidence of his own frustration showed in his voice.

Emily shrugged her thin shoulders and he thought how like Isobel she was. Her hair was lighter, of course, and at present her childish features only hinted that one day she might possess her mother's beauty. But she was tall and slender, and her eyes were the same luminous shade of blue.

'Granny sent for her,' she answered at last. Then, as if compelled to make the compromise, 'She's not very well.'

A curse slipped out before he could prevent it, but the only reaction Emily made was to arch her brows in a reproof that was uncannily like her grandmother's. 'So you've no idea when she'll be back?'

Emily hesitated. 'Well—she said she wouldn't be long,' she muttered unwillingly.

'Wait a minute.' Jake had just had a thought. 'Are you on your own?'

'What's it to you?' Emily resumed her defiant attitude. 'I'm not a baby, you know.'

'Maybe not.' Jake scowled. 'But even a ten-year-old should know better than to open the door to a stranger.'

'Actually, I'm almost eleven,' Emily corrected him scornfully. 'Not that I'd expect you to remember that. You're just my father.'

'I am not your—'

Jake broke off abruptly. He refused to get into an argument with her about her parentage. He didn't know why the hell Isobel had told her he was her father, unless it was her way of shifting the blame. It was certainly true that it had caused an unbreakable rift between him and her daughter. And any hope he might have had of making an ally of the child had been stymied by her lies.

'Anyway, I knew it was you,' Emily added carelessly. 'I saw you out of the window.' Her eyes surveyed him with a surprisingly adult appraisal. 'You're wet.'

Jake's jaw compressed. 'You noticed,' he said drily, glancing down at his rain-spotted jacket. 'Yeah, you may have observed that it's raining.'

'Peeing it down,' agreed Emily, with a calculated effort to shock. 'I s'pose you'd better come in.'

Jake hesitated. 'Did your mother tell you I was coming?' he demanded, suddenly sensing why she'd been looking out of the window. He wondered if it also explained Isobel's willingness to leave her daughter alone while she travelled across London at the start of the rush hour. My God, did she expect him to stay until she got back? To act as Emily's babysitter, no less?

'She might have done,' Emily responded indifferently, turning and walking away from him. She paused halfway down the hall and looked back at him. 'Are you coming in or not?'

Or not, thought Jake savagely, glancing at the narrow gold watch on his wrist and stifling an oath. It was already after five. He'd promised Marcie he'd pick her up from her hairdresser's in Mayfair at six. Dammit, he wasn't going to make it.

He heard the sound of a door opening downstairs and looked hopefully over the banister. But it was only one of the other tenants, probably arriving home from work. Suppressing his anger, he stepped unwillingly into his wife's apartment.

Emily had already taken his acceptance for granted and disappeared into a room at the end of the hall. If Jake's memory served him correctly it was the kitchen, and, shrugging out of his wet jacket, he shouldered the outer door closed and followed her.

As he'd expected, Emily was in the kitchen, filling the kettle at the sink and plugging it in.

'I expect you'd like some coffee,' she said, her cool detachment reminding him again of her mother. 'I'm afraid it's only instant. Mummy says we can't afford anything else.'

Jake gritted his teeth as he slung his jacket onto a vacant stool. The casual aside had really got to him. Why couldn't they afford anything else? He'd paid Isobel enough over the years, goodness knew.

But it wasn't something he wanted to take up with the child, and he watched from between lowered lids as Emily spooned coffee into a china mug. She was evidently used to the task. She cast a glance in his direction as she took a jug of milk from the fridge.

'Do you take milk and sugar?' she asked politely, and Jake blew out an exasperated breath.

'I didn't say I wanted anything,' he said shortly. Then, unwillingly, 'Ought you to be handling boiling water?'

'Oh, please!' Emily gave him a cynical look. 'Don't pretend you care what happens to me.' The luminous blue eyes dismissed his concern. 'And, as it happens, I'm perfectly capable of making tea or coffee. I've been doing it for ages.'

Jake's jaw compressed. 'If you say so.'

'I do say so.' Emily braced herself against the counter, arms spread out to either side. 'So—what do you want?'

'Like I'm going to tell a precocious little girl like you,' retorted Jake, resenting her tone. 'When did your mother leave?'

Emily shrugged. 'A little while ago.'

'How little a while ago?'

'I don't know.' She put up her hand and pulled her plait over one shoulder. 'An hour, maybe.'

'An hour?'

Jake felt slightly reassured. By his reckoning, it should take Isobel no more than an hour to reach the service flat in Bayswater. She'd spend—what?—maybe half an hour with her mother before coming back? Two and a half hours in all. Which meant he would be too late to pick Marcie up as he'd expected, but not too late to make their dinner engagement with the Allens.

'You didn't say how you liked your coffee.'

While he'd been mulling over his options the kettle had boiled and Emily had filled the mug with boiling water. 'I—as it comes,' he muttered, deciding there was no point in complaining now that the coffee was made. 'Thanks,' he added, when she pushed the mug towards him. His lips twisted. 'Aren't you joining me?'

'I don't drink coffee,' said Emily, hesitating a moment before leading the way into the adjoining living room. 'We might as well go in here.'

Jake arched his brows, but, picking up his jacket and his coffee, he followed her. She was right. He might as well make himself comfortable. They both knew he wasn't going anywhere until Isobel got home.

The living room was the largest room in the apartment. When Isobel had moved in she'd furnished it in a manner that suited the high ceilings and polished wood floors. Instead of modern chairs and sofas she'd chosen a pair of mahogany-framed settees and two high-backed armchairs upholstered in burgundy velvet. There were several occasional tables and a carved oak cabinet containing the china and silverware her mother had given them as a wedding present. A tall bookcase, crammed with books, flanked the Adam-style fireplace, where Isobel's only concession to the twenty-first century smouldered behind a glass screen. But an open fire would have been too dangerous with a young child in the apartment, and the gas replacement was very convincing.

Long velvet curtains hung at the broad bay windows, their dark rose colour faded to a muted shade. The huge rug that occupied the centre of the floor was faded, too, and Jake wondered if that was a deliberate choice. Goodness knew, with the money he paid her every month—and her job—she shouldn't be hard up.

But as he looked about him he noticed there were definite signs of wear and tear about the place. The cabinets were in need of attention and the polished floor was scuffed. Was Isobel finding it too much, juggling a job and looking after her home and family?

Determined not to feel in any way responsible for Isobel's problems, Jake draped his jacket over the back of a chair. Then, lounging onto one of the sofas, he hooked an ankle across his knee. The coffee was too hot to drink at present, so he set the mug on the floor beside him.

He should have known better, he reflected, as Emily hustled across the room to set an end table beside him. She placed a coaster on it and bent to pick up his mug, but he forestalled her. 'I'll do it,' he said, containing his impatience. 'You can go and do your homework or whatever it is you usually do at this time of the afternoon.'

But Emily apparently had no intention of leaving him on his own. 'I can do my homework later,' she said, seating herself in the armchair across the hearth from him. 'I've got plenty of time.'

But I haven't, thought Jake drily, regarding the girl through exasperated eyes. She was certainly Isobel's daughter, he reflected, noticing the way she sat with her back straight, her knees demurely drawn together. Or perhaps that was a result of her grandmother's teaching. The old lady had certainly influenced Isobel. Why shouldn't she influence her granddaughter, too?

At least his scrutiny appeared to be getting through to her. She was still wearing the grey skirt, white blouse and dark green cardigan she wore for school, and now she averted her eyes, poking a finger through one of the buttonholes on the cardigan. Was she nervous of him? he wondered, feeling a reluctant trace of sympathy at the thought. Dammit, what lies had Isobel told her about him?

'So,' he said, feeling obliged to say something, 'what's wrong with your grandma?'

'*Granny's* not well,' she repeated, not too nervous to take the opportunity to correct him. 'I told you that.'

'Yeah, but what's wrong with her?' asked Jake shortly. 'Do you know?'

Emily compressed her small mouth. 'I think—I think it's something to do with her heart,' she responded at last. Then, with more confidence, 'She had an operation last year.'

'Did she?'

Jake frowned. Isobel had told him nothing about that. But then, why would she? They hardly ever saw one another these days.

'You don't like Granny, do you?' Emily remarked suddenly, and Jake caught his breath.

'I beg your pardon?'

'You don't like Granny,' Emily reiterated blandly. 'She says you never did.'

'Does she?' Jake was aware of an anger out of all proportion to the offence. 'Well, she'd know, I suppose.'

'Why?' Emily arched enquiring eyebrows and Jake sighed.

'I guess because she never liked me,' he replied after a moment's consideration. Why shouldn't he defend himself? The old girl had had it her own way long enough. 'I dare say she didn't tell you that.'

'No.' Emily looked doubtful. 'Is that why you don't live with us any more?'

'No!' Jake knew he sounded resentful and he quickly modified his tone. 'Look, why don't you go and watch TV or something? I've got some calls to make.'

Emily frowned. 'What calls?'

'Phone calls,' said Jake shortly, getting to his feet and pulling his cellphone out of his jacket pocket. 'Do you mind?'

'I don't mind.' Emily shook her head. 'Who are you going to call?'

My mistress?

Jake tried the answer on for size and instantly rejected it. His quarrel had never been with the child, after all. She was the innocent victim here and he had no desire to hurt her.

'A friend,' he said instead, sitting down again. 'No one you know.'

'A woman-friend?'

Emily was persistent, and once again Jake had to guard his tongue.

'Does it matter?' he asked, maintaining a neutral tone with an effort. He paused significantly. 'Can I have a little privacy here?'

'*May* I have a little privacy,' Emily corrected him primly. 'Granny says you keep beans in cans.'

Granny had far too much to say for herself, thought Jake

savagely. But he was relieved when Emily got to her feet and started towards to the door.

'I'll go and see what we're having for supper,' she said with evident reluctance. 'It's probably going be late when Mummy gets back.'

Jake opened his mouth to say it had better not be, and then closed it again. Emily had left the room in any case. Besides, he was half convinced she'd only been baiting him. For a ten—*almost eleven*—year-old, she was remarkably mature.

Marcie sounded less than pleased when she came on the line. 'Don't tell me,' she said. 'You're going to be late. Honestly, Jake, I thought you said it wouldn't take long.'

Jake sighed. He could hear the sounds of the hair salon in the background: the constant buzz of voices, the hum of the driers, the subtle Muzak that was supposed to relax the clients.

'There's been a complication,' he said, hoping she could hear him. 'Isobel's not here.'

'She's not there?' Obviously she could hear him loud and clear. 'So what's the problem? You'll have to see her some other time.'

'No, I can't. That is—' Jake knew it wasn't going to be easy convincing her that he had to stay. 'Emily's here.'

'The kid?'

'Isobel's daughter, yes.' Jake didn't really like the dismissive way Marcie had spoken of her. 'She's on her own.'

'So?'

'So I've got to stay until her mother gets back,' said Jake evenly. 'You'd better order a cab to take you home from the salon.'

'No!' Marcie sounded furious. 'Jake, do you have any idea how difficult it is to order a cab at this time of the evening?'

'I know.' Jake blew out a weary breath. 'I'm sorry. But there's nothing I can do.'

'There *is* something you can do,' she retorted angrily. 'You can leave your wife's bastard on her own and get over here and pick me up like you promised.'

'Don't call her that!' Jake couldn't prevent the automatic reproof. 'For God's sake, Marcie, she's not to blame because Isobel's gone to her mother's.'

'And nor am I,' responded Marcie grimly. 'Come on, Jake, you know she's trying it on. She probably guessed how you'd feel when you found—Emily—on her own.'

'She didn't have a lot of choice,' said Jake, wondering why he was defending his wife to his girlfriend. 'The old lady's ill, apparently. I guess it could be her heart.'

'My heart bleeds.' Marcie snorted, but then, as if realising how unsympathetic she sounded, she took a deep breath. 'Okay,' she said, capitulating, 'I'll take a cab home. And you'll pick me up in—what? An hour and a half?'

'Something like that,' agreed Jake, glancing at his watch. Surely Isobel would be back by half-past six.

'You haven't forgotten we're going out this evening, have you, Jake?' Marcie had heard the unspoken doubt in his voice and reacted to it. 'You'll need at least an hour to shower and change.'

'I know that.' Jake was beginning to feel harassed. 'Back off, will you, Marcie? I'll be there.'

'Oh, Jake.' Marcie groaned. 'I'm sorry if I sound like a bitch. I've just been looking forward to this evening so much. I haven't spent the best part of the day in the beauty salon to have—well, to have Isobel spoil it.'

'She won't spoil it. I promise.' Jake hoped he wasn't making promises he couldn't keep. 'Gotta go now. I'll see you later.'

He didn't give her a chance to argue. Out of the corner of his eye he'd glimpsed Emily hovering just beyond the doorway into the kitchen, and he had no intention of providing her with any juicy gossip to relay to her mother.

As soon as he'd flipped the phone closed she showed herself, however. 'Finished?' she asked, and he nodded, wondering if he was being naïve in thinking she hadn't been listening all along.

But it was too late to do anything about it now and, picking up his coffee, he took a grateful gulp. Thankfully, it was cool enough to drink, and surprisingly good besides. Clearly she hadn't been exaggerating when she'd said she'd done it before.

'Would you like some more?' she asked as he set down the empty mug, but Jake declined.

'Not right now,' he said, and as she turned away to return the mug to the kitchen he found himself watching her with a curiously critical eye.

In her school uniform, she could have been any one of the hundred or so children who attended the Lady Stafford Middle School. But, despite himself, Jake knew he'd have no difficulty in picking her out of a crowd. Although he'd only seen her a handful of times in the past ten years, he'd have recognised her anywhere, and if it hadn't been so annoying it would have been pathetic.

Dammit, she wasn't his daughter. She had never been his daughter, and if Isobel hadn't been so hell-bent on lying to her, he and the child might well have achieved a friendly relationship. As it was, Emily hated him and he resented her.

She came back then, resuming her seat opposite him, and rather than suffer the discomfort of another prolonged appraisal Jake chose another tack.

'So, what do you do in your spare time?' he asked pleasantly. 'Do you have a computer?'

'Of course I have a computer. Everybody does.'

Emily was scathing, and Jake tried again. 'How about

computer games?' he suggested. 'I'm pretty good at them myself.'

'You play computer games?'

She couldn't keep the scorn out of her voice, and Jake felt an unwilling sense of indignation. Evidently Isobel had been selective in choosing what information to give the child, and he would enjoy exploding her bubble.

'I invent them,' he said flatly. 'Among other things. Didn't your mother tell you?'

'No.' There was a reluctant glimmer of interest in Emily's eyes. 'What games have you invented?'

Jake frowned, pretending to think. 'Let me see,' he said thoughtfully. 'Have you heard of Moonraider? Space Spirals? Black Knights?'

Emily's jaw had dropped. 'You invented Black Knights?' she exclaimed incredulously. 'I don't believe it.'

Jake shrugged. 'You've played it, then?'

'Yes. Yes.' Emily glanced over her shoulder. 'Mummy bought me a Dreambox for Christmas.'

Jake pulled a wry face. 'That was good of her.'

'Why? Oh, God!' Emily pressed both hands to her cheeks. 'Did you invent Dreambox?'

'I own Dreambox,' Jake told her ruefully. 'And I don't think your mother would approve of you saying "Oh, God", do you?'

'Granny would report me to Father Joseph,' agreed Emily, pulling a face. 'I'd probably have to say a hundred Hail Marys for taking the Lord's name in vain. But still—' She stared at him admiringly. 'You own Dreambox! Cool!'

Jake was surprised at how flattered he was by her reaction. She was only a child, but the hero-worship in her eyes felt good. He was genuinely pleased that she approved of him. It made him want to go out and buy her every game he'd marketed to date.

'You wouldn't—like—play Black Knights with me?' she

suggested suddenly. 'Just till Mummy gets back, I mean. It would give us something to do.'

Jake hesitated. He had the feeling Isobel would not approve of this development. Okay, maybe she'd had some crazy idea that if she threw him and Emily together he might change his mind about her. But the arrangement had to be on her terms, not his.

To hell with that!

Looking at the girl's expectant face, he made a gesture of acceptance. 'Why not?' he said, getting to his feet again. 'Where's your computer? In your room?'

Some time later, when Jake's cellphone began to ring, he was shocked to find it was nearly seven o'clock. He'd been so absorbed in the game, which he'd discovered Emily played extremely well, that he'd forgotten the time. Dodging witches and goblins, vaulting over chasms where dragons lurked, laughing at the obstacles someone's vivid imagination had created, he'd realised how much fun it was to play with someone who genuinely wanted to beat him. Apart from his second-in-command at McCabe Tectonics, everyone else he employed seemed keener on winning his approval than winning the game.

With a word of apology to the child, he strode back into the living room, where he'd left the phone, and glanced at the small screen with some misgivings. As he'd expected, it was Marcie's number displayed there and she wasn't pleased. 'Where are you?' she demanded. 'I thought you were picking me up at seven o'clock.'

'Seven-thirty,' he amended, not knowing why he'd bothered making the distinction. Even if he left now, he wasn't going to make it.

'Okay, half-past seven,' she conceded irritably. 'So, are you on your way? I know you're not at the house. I already tried there.'

Right.

Jake expelled a weary breath, and as he did so he heard the sound of Isobel's key in the lock.

Well, it had to be Isobel, he mused blackly, aware that she couldn't have chosen a more awkward time to return. Here he was, trying to placate his girlfriend, with his wife as an unwilling audience.

CHAPTER TWO

EMILY came into the room at that moment, too. She must have heard Isobel, and she bounded eagerly across the living room to meet her.

'Daddy and I have been playing computer games,' she exclaimed, by way of a greeting, and Jake didn't have time to cover the mouthpiece of his phone before Marcie latched on to the anomaly.

'*Daddy* and I?' she spat angrily. 'What's going on, Jake? I thought you said you weren't the kid's father.'

'I'm not.'

Jake balked before saying anything more with his wife regarding him from the hall doorway. Dammit, there was no easy way to do this. Whatever he said, he was going to offend somebody.

'Jake.' Isobel was civil enough, but he could see the strain in her face. 'It was good of you to stay.'

Yeah, right.

Jake bit back the sardonic response, giving her a brief nod of acknowledgement as Marcie spoke again. 'Is Isobel there?' she demanded. 'Jake—'

'Look, I've got to go,' he interrupted her, aware that he was building up trouble for himself later, but unable to do anything about it right now. 'Take a cab to the hotel, will you? I'll join you there as soon as I can.'

'Jake—'

'Just do it,' he said tightly, and felt a momentary pang of remorse when she rang off without saying another word.

Flipping his phone closed, he was aware that Isobel was still watching him. 'I'm sorry if we've upset your dinner

21

arrangements,' she said stiffly. 'I was as quick as I could be, but my mother isn't well.'

'I'm sorry.'

It was a standard response and her lips twisted a little wryly at his words. 'Yes—well, that's not your problem.' Her face softened as she looked at Emily. 'I hope you've been a good girl.'

Emily grimaced. 'I'm not a baby, Mummy. Like I said before, Daddy and I have been playing Black Knights.' Her face brightened. 'He owns Dreambox. Did you know that?'

Isobel's lips thinned. 'Yes. He's very clever,' she said drily, unbuttoning her navy overcoat and unwinding a silk scarf from around her neck. 'Now, why don't you go and make me some tea, Em? I think—' She looked questioningly at Jake. 'I think we have to talk.'

Emily pulled a face. 'Do I have to?'

'Em!'

'Oh, all right.'

Emily flounced out of the room and Isobel finished taking off her coat. Underneath, she was wearing a cream silk shirt and a navy skirt that ended an inch or two above her knees, but Jake barely noticed. What disturbed him was how thin she had become; the bones of her shoulders were clearly evident beneath the thin fabric of her shirt.

Yet she was still beautiful, he reflected unwillingly. The pale oval of her face was framed by ebony-dark hair, drawn back from a centre parting and secured in a loose chignon at her nape. Luminous blue eyes and high cheekbones only emphasised the generous width of her mouth, and her porcelain skin gave her a fleeting resemblance to the Madonna.

But Jake knew she was no saint. Isobel was—had always been—a warm, passionate woman, and although he despised her for the way she'd treated him, he had never lost his admiration for her grace and elegance.

Now, however, he was concerned by her appearance, and

with the comments that Emily had made still ringing his ears he said abruptly, 'Is there something you're not telling me?'

Isobel carefully folded her coat and laid it over a chair. 'I don't know what you mean,' she said, avoiding his eyes. Then, straightening, 'I'm sorry you've had to hang about, but there was nothing I could do. Mama phoned and…'

Her voice trailed away and Jake's mouth compressed. 'And you couldn't let her down,' he remarked sardonically. 'Tell me something new.'

Isobel's lips tightened. 'You don't understand. She's been extremely—fragile—since her—well, in recent months.'

'Since her operation, you mean?' Jake regarded her with cynical eyes. 'Emily told me.'

'I see.' Isobel hesitated. 'Then you'll know that by-pass operations on the elderly can have—complications.'

'So that's what it was.' Jake nodded. 'I didn't know.'

Isobel frowned. 'But you said—Emily—'

'She was pretty vague.' He shrugged, and then glanced about him. 'Look, why don't you sit down? You look tired.'

'Thanks.'

It was hardly a compliment, but Isobel was glad to accept his advice. She was tired; exhausted, actually. She had been for weeks; months. Ever since she'd heard that her husband was involved with Marcie Duncan.

Of course, he'd had affairs before. Several, actually, over the years, and she'd suffered through every one of them. But his relationship with Marcie was something different. It had gone on for so much longer, for one thing, and for another a friend had told her that Marcie was telling everyone that he was going to marry her.

Except he was still married to Isobel.

Expelling a quivering breath, she moved into the room

and seated herself on the sofa nearest to the door. Then, as he lounged into the chair opposite, she forced a formal smile.

But it was difficult. *Bloody* difficult, actually, she thought with a sudden spurt of anger. Sitting opposite the man you had once thought you loved better than life itself was never going to be easy, and she despised the fact that he could come here and behave as if all they had ever been to one another was polite strangers.

He looked so damned relaxed, she mused tensely. In the kind of casual gear he wore to work, which her mother had always deplored on a man in his position, he looked completely at his ease and she resented it.

A black tee shirt was stretched across his broad shoulders and exposed the ribbed muscles of his stomach. He didn't appear to have an ounce of spare flesh on him, and tight-fitting moleskin pants hugged his narrow hips and long powerful legs. A leather jacket, still displaying the fact that it had been raining when he arrived, was hung over the back of a chair and one booted foot rested casually across his knee.

He was not a handsome man, she assured herself, unwilling to admit that his strong, hard features possessed something more than mere good looks. His skin was darker than the rest of his colouring, his hair streaked in shades of silvery blond and amber, and eyes as green as his Irish roots should have indicated a fair countenance. But somewhere in Jake's mongrel ancestry—as her mother would say—there had been a darker strain. Just another reason why Lady Hannah Lacey had opposed his marriage to her only daughter.

'Have you been waiting long?' she asked at last, rather than broach the subject she was sure was his reason for being here, and Jake regarded her through narrowed lids.

'What do you think?' he asked. 'Our appointment was for five o'clock, wasn't it?'

Isobel sighed. 'Do we have to have appointments?' She smoothed her damp palms over the slim lines of her skirt. 'This isn't a business meeting, is it?'

Jake didn't answer that. Instead, he said, 'I guess you know why I'm here,' and a shiver feathered its way down her spine.

'Do I?' She refused to make it easy for him. 'Dare I suspect that you've finally decided to acknowledge that you have a daughter?'

'No!' Jake's appearance of relaxation disappeared. His boot thudded onto the carpet and he leaned forward in his seat, legs spread wide, forearms resting along his thighs. 'We dealt with that fiction some time ago, and I don't intend to let you divert me with it now. I'm here because it's past time we put an end to this travesty—'

'What are we having for supper, Mummy?'

Isobel didn't know if Emily had been eavesdropping on their conversation or whether her intervention was as innocent as it appeared. Either way, it achieved the dual purpose of providing a distraction and putting Jake off his stride.

He swore, quite audibly, and Isobel glared at him reprovingly before transferring her attention to her daughter. 'Have you made the tea?' she asked, ignoring her husband's scowling face. 'We can decide what we're having for supper later.'

'Will Daddy be staying for supper?'

Emily was nothing if not persistent, and despite everything Isobel was tempted to smile. 'I doubt it,' she said. 'Just fetch the tea, sweetheart. Then you can go and start running your bath.'

'Oh, must I?'

'Do as your mother says,' said Jake harshly, and Emily's expression changed from mild disappointment to cold fury.

'Don't you tell me what to do, you—you womaniser!' she exclaimed angrily, and Isobel didn't know which of them was the most astounded at her outburst.

After the way Emily had behaved when she'd got home Isobel had hoped that she and Jake had come to some sort of compromise. She should have known better.

Predictably, Jake recovered first. 'You little bitch!' he snapped. 'How dare you call me a womaniser?'

'Because it's what you are,' declared Emily, unwilling to back down, and Jake snorted.

'I bet you got that from your grandmother, didn't you?' he demanded. 'That old—'

'I heard it at school, actually,' Emily contradicted him, her voice breaking a little now. 'It's what the older girls say about you. They laugh about it. They say you've had loads of girlfriends and that you don't care about Mummy and me at all.'

Isobel didn't know where to look. It was obvious that the child's words had shocked her husband, but she knew she couldn't allow Emily to get away with insolence, whatever the justification.

'I think you owe your father an apology, Emily,' she said quietly, uncaring what Jake thought of her words. But his response overrode hers.

'I don't care what people say,' he retorted grimly, but Isobel could tell from his tone that that wasn't entirely true. Jake was not without feelings, after all, and Emily's accusations had the ring of truth. 'Your mother knows I would never allow her—or you—to suffer from my actions.'

'But we do,' muttered Emily tearfully. 'Why can't we be a proper family? Why can't you live with us, like any proper father would?'

'Emily—'

Isobel was desperate to stop this from going any further, but Jake had had enough.

'Because I'm *not* your father,' he snapped savagely, and Isobel closed her eyes as Emily's face whitened and the tears began to fall in earnest.

'You are,' she protested, in spite of her distress, and although Isobel got to her feet and started towards her it was too late. 'I know you are,' she persisted. 'Mummy says so. And Mummy doesn't tell lies.

'And nor do I,' said Jake, driven to his feet also. 'For pity's sake, Emily—'

'I don't want to listen to you.' Emily put both hands over her ears and stared at him through tear-drenched lashes. 'I *am* your daughter. You know I am.' She turned despairingly towards Isobel. 'Tell him, Mummy. Tell him that's who I am. He has to believe you. Especially today.'

Isobel managed to get an arm about her daughter's shoulders, but Jake wasn't finished. 'What do you mean?' he asked suspiciously. 'Why especially today?'

'Because of the game,' said Emily tremulously. 'Because of Black Knights. You said it yourself. You said I was like you. I played to win.'

It was at least forty minutes before Isobel returned to find Jake pacing about the living room like a caged lion. His eyes turned instantly to her as soon as she appeared in the doorway, and she could tell from the stark lines that etched his mouth that he had been fighting his own demons since she'd led the weeping child away.

'How is she?' he demanded, pausing on the hearth, and because he was back-lit by the orange flames of the fire his face was partly in shadow.

'How do you think?' Isobel wasn't inclined to reassure him, even if it wasn't all his fault that Emily had got so upset. Then, reluctantly, she added, 'She's gone to sleep.

Finally. She was exhausted.' She paused. 'I'm surprised you're still here.'

Jake's jaw tightened. 'Where else would I be?'

'Oh, right.' Isobel's nostrils flared in sudden comprehension. 'We never did finish our conversation, did we?'

Jake bit off an oath. 'That's not why I stayed.'

'No?' Isobel felt too weary to cope with anything just now. She glanced at her watch and was astonished to find it was after half-past-eight. 'Goodness, is that the time?'

'You didn't even get that cup of tea,' remarked Jake wryly. 'I could do with a drink myself. How do you feel about me making us both one?'

'I can do it.' The last thing Isobel wanted was for Jake to feel he had to look after her. It would be far too ironic. 'I assume you'd prefer something stronger than tea? All I've got is sherry, I'm afraid.'

'No beer?'

'I don't like beer,' said Isobel stiffly. 'And I can't aff— I mean, we have no use for spirits.'

Jake's mouth tightened, and she guessed he knew exactly what she had been going to say. But, although she prepared herself for an argument, all he said was, 'How about cola? Surely Emily drinks that?'

'Diet cola,' agreed Isobel, starting towards the kitchen. 'I think we've got some in the fridge.'

Jake followed her, his hands pushed into his hip pockets, his hair rumpled, as if he had spent some of the time he'd been waiting running his fingers through it. Yet he still looked as attractive as ever, and Isobel thought how unfair it was that one man should continue to have such power over her.

But it was dangerous thinking about that now, and she busied herself taking a can of cola from the fridge, setting it and a glass on the counter nearest to him. Then, switching on the kettle, she emptied the pot of tea Emily had made earlier.

Jake didn't touch the glass. He simply flipped the tab and drank straight from the can, his head tipped back, the muscles in his throat moving rhythmically as he swallowed the chilled liquid.

Isobel found herself watching him and quickly looked away. But in her mind's eye she could still see the smooth column of his throat and the brown skin that disappeared into the neckline of his tee shirt.

He seemed darker-skinned than usual, and she wondered where he had spent his winter break this year. Then she remembered. There had been an article in one of the tabloids about how ex-Page Three model Marcie Duncan had been seen holidaying with her latest conquest, computer millionaire Jake McCabe, in the Seychelles.

There had been pictures, too, but Isobel hadn't looked at those. She wouldn't have seen the article at all if Lady Hannah hadn't saved it for her. She winced. Sometimes she couldn't make up her mind whether her mother truly had her best interests at heart or if she got some perverted kind of pleasure out of proving that she had been right all along.

'Thanks.'

While she had been wool-gathering Jake had finished the can, and now he crushed it in his fist before dropping it into the swing bin beside the sink.

Isobel forced herself to concentrate on what she was doing. 'Do you want another?' she asked, grateful that the kettle had boiled and she could make her tea. Her legs felt decidedly wobbly and she would be glad when she could sit down.

'Not right now.' Jake shifted restlessly as she put milk into a mug and filled it from the pot. Then, in a low voice, 'I guess I should apologise.'

Isobel tried not to show her surprise. Flicking him an

uncertain glance, she moved past him into the living room again. 'If you mean it,' she said at last, resuming the seat she'd occupied earlier on the sofa. She sipped her tea. 'Mmm, I was ready for this.'

She was aware that Jake was still standing in the doorway behind her, and she wished she could see his face. Or perhaps not, she amended. She had never been able to hide her feelings from him.

When her nerves felt as if they'd been stretched to breaking point he moved into the room, but instead of sitting in the armchair, as before, he joined her on the couch.

'I mean it,' he said, his weight depressing the cushion beside her. 'I didn't mean to blurt it out like that. But, dammit, Belle, I thought she knew.'

Isobel steeled herself to look at him. 'Knew what?' she asked, though she knew exactly what he meant.

Jake blew out a breath. 'That I'm not her father,' he declared harshly. 'If you insist on having me say it yet again.'

Isobel's dark brows ascended. 'But you *are* her father,' she said, as she had said so many times before. 'You just don't want to believe it.'

'Damn right.' He sounded angry. 'For God's sake, Isobel, how long are you going to persist with this—this fabrication?'

Isobel put her mug down on the table beside her. 'As long as it takes, I suppose,' she replied, amazed that she could sound so cool when inside she was burning up. Then, realising that she couldn't delay the moment any longer, she lifted her shoulders in a wary gesture. 'Why don't you tell me why you wanted to see me?'

Jake stared at her, his eyes as vivid as jade in his dark face. 'Do you think it's fair on Emily to give her unreal expectations?' he demanded, without answering her, and Isobel sighed.

'You mean because her father refuses to acknowledge her?' she asked tersely. 'I don't think so.'

Jake's jaw hardened. 'Dammit, she's not my child!'

'She is.'

'How can you say that? When you and Piers Mallory were having an affair at the time?'

Isobel pursed her lips. 'We were not having an affair!'

'You slept with him.'

'I was in bed with him,' she said, annoyed to find her voice was shaking. 'But not through choice.'

Jake snorted. 'Oh, right. Are you saying he raped you now?'

'No.' Isobel picked up her tea again, endeavouring to warm her frozen hands on the mug. 'But I'd been drinking. I don't remember anything about it.'

With an oath Jake got up from the sofa and paced grimly across the rug. His powerful frame cast a long shadow across the hearth and she turned to stare into the flames of the gas fire rather than look at him. But the temptation to do so was almost irresistible, and only the fact that the hot liquid was burning her palms caused her to turn her attention to putting the mug down again.

'He was my friend,' said Jake, speaking through his teeth, and Isobel felt the familiar frustration building inside her.

'Yes, I know,' she said. 'That was the trouble, wasn't it? You couldn't believe *your* friend could do something so—so—'

'Unlikely?' suggested Jake scornfully, but Isobel shook her head.

'So despicable,' she corrected, looking up at him with accusing eyes. 'And on that basis you decided that Emily couldn't possibly be your daughter. That she was his.'

Jake blew out a breath. 'I don't want to talk about this.'

'I'll bet.'

'For God's sake, Belle, be honest for once in your life!' Jake came to stand in front of her and she averted her eyes from the impressive bulge of his manhood. 'We'd been married for three years, dammit, and you hadn't got pregnant. Are you telling me we suddenly got lucky? I don't think so.'

'We'd been trying to avoid me getting pregnant,' cried Isobel fiercely. 'You know that.'

'But accidents happen. That's what you said, isn't it?'

Isobel groaned. 'Well, what are you saying?' she demanded, putting out a hand as if to ward him off. 'That Piers Mallory is so—so macho that one night with him was enough?'

'If it *was* just one night,' retorted Jake harshly. 'And I only have your word for that.'

Isobel couldn't sit still any longer. Trembling violently, she got to her feet, pushing him aside and stumbling away from the sofa. Of course he only had her word for it. Piers was never going to admit what he'd done.

'In any case, your getting pregnant was just adding insult to injury,' said Jake heavily, and there was a trace of bitterness in his voice now. 'How could you do it, Belle? How could you have an affair with my best friend? God, you knew how I'd feel about it. Piers and I had been friends since we started college.'

Isobel gripped the back of a chair for support, her nails digging into the fabric as she struggled to regain control. 'Piers was never your friend, Jake,' she said, ignoring his immediate growl of derision. 'He wasn't. He was jealous of you, of our life together. He'd have done anything to split us up.'

'That's crap and you know it.' Jake was scathing. 'I don't know why you keep repeating the same old story, the same old lies. It's not as if I haven't heard it all before.'

Isobel held up her head. 'I suppose I'm hoping that one

day you'll come to your senses and believe me,' she replied huskily. 'That you'll at least consider that Emily might be your daughter.'

'She's not,' said Jake flatly. 'She's nothing like me.'

'She's nothing like Piers Mallory either,' retorted Isabel, feeling the familiar wave of despair creeping over her. 'For pity's sake, Jake, when have I ever lied to you?'

'When you told me that you and Piers had never slept together,' Jake responded at once. 'You were pretty convincing then.'

'Because it's true.'

'But you're not denying he was making love to you when I found you?'

Isobel's shoulders sagged. 'He was trying to, yes.'

'Right.' Jake regarded her contemptuously. 'So why do you persist in saying you never had sex with him?'

Isobel shook her head. 'I don't believe I did. In any case, I was—afraid.'

'Afraid of me?'

'Afraid of what would happen if you believed I'd been unfaithful to you,' she moaned miserably. 'I knew how you'd react.'

'You weren't wrong.' Jake gave a weary shake of his head. 'And you told me you didn't even like him.'

'I didn't.'

But Isobel knew she was fighting a losing battle. It was a battle she'd been fighting and losing for the past eleven years, and nothing she said or did was going to change Jake's mind now.

'It's getting late,' he said abruptly. 'And you look exhausted, never mind Emily. I'd better go.'

Isobel stared at him. 'But we haven't talked.'

'No.' he was sardonic. 'Well, not about anything that matters anyway.' He paused. 'I'll come back another day. When I've got more time and you're not dead beat.'

Isobel's lips twisted. 'You certainly know how to flatter a girl, Jake. I'd forgotten how charming you can be.'

'You don't need me to flatter you, Isobel.' Jake swung his jacket off the chair and shouldered his way into it. Then, almost reluctantly, he added, 'You know how bloody attractive you are. You always have. I guess that was why I found it so hard to trust you. I knew it was only a matter of time before you found some other mug to add a little excitement to our marriage.'

CHAPTER THREE

JAKE was at his desk by eight o'clock the next morning.

He could have been there much earlier. He hadn't been to bed. He'd spent most of the night switching channels on the too-large digital TV Marcie had insisted he should install in his bedroom, and which he'd actually set up in the den, trying not to think about the row they'd had at her apartment when she'd got back from dining with the Allens—alone.

But then, that was what happened when you allowed your soon-to-be-ex-wife to ruin what should have been a very pleasant evening, he reflected ruefully. Frank Allen and his wife were old friends of his, and he knew Marcie had been relying on him to persuade the media tycoon to back her bid for network stardom.

She'd already done some TV work, appearing on chat shows, celebrity quizzes and the like, but she wanted to be taken seriously. She wanted to bury her bimbette image once and for all, and make her name with her own daytime talk show.

It had been a long shot at best. Jake knew that. Frank Allen hadn't been in the business for more than forty years without being able to spot an amateur when he saw one. Marcie looked good on panel shows, when her contribution meant less to the producers than her appearance, but she simply didn't have what it took to take centre stage.

Jake had suggested she ought to consider acting lessons, but Marcie had quickly vetoed that idea. She hadn't become the most successful photographic model of the decade by admitting she didn't have what it took to further her career.

She didn't want to hear that she needed more than good looks to make it in the very competitive world of television. Because other people had done it, she confidently believed that she could do it, too.

She had taken the fact that Jake hadn't turned up at the restaurant as a personal slight. Even though he'd sent a message to both Marcie and Frank Allen—in Marcie's case enclosed with an enormous bouquet of red roses, which he'd had the devil's own job to acquire at half-past nine at night—explaining that he'd been inadvertently held up and apologising for letting them down, she'd still been furious.

Finding him waiting for her at her apartment when she'd returned home had not placated her. She'd virtually thrown the bouquet at him, declaring that he'd deliberately ruined the evening, that he cared more for his estranged wife and her snotty-nosed brat than he did about her.

There had been no reasoning with her, and Jake had eventually scooped up the bouquet and left the apartment. He'd deposited the roses in the nearest wastebin. He'd been angry, too, but whether it had been with himself or her he hadn't cared to speculate.

Which was why he was at his desk before the rest of the staff turned in, scowling at his computer screen, wishing last night had never happened. And not just because of the row with Marcie. They'd had rows before, and no doubt would again. That was a given in their relationship. But because last night for the first time he'd learned that Isobel's daughter had a wit and a personality all her own.

Until then he'd hardly spoken to the child. His dealings with her mother had been brief at best, and his memories of Emily were of a shy toddler, hiding behind Isobel's skirts, or a sulky pre-teen, who'd resented his presence.

Well, she'd resented his presence last night, too, he conceded. To begin with, anyway. But afterwards, after they'd discovered a common interest in computer games, she'd become almost friendly. She'd actually laughed at his efforts to keep up with her, and he'd felt an unexpected surge of admiration at her ability to keep two steps ahead.

That was why he felt so bad about what had come after, he thought now, stabbing savagely at the keys. Dammit, he hadn't meant to hurt the kid. It wasn't his fault that Isobel had never told Emily the truth, but he'd felt bloody guilty when she'd got so upset.

Which was the real reason why he hadn't joined Marcie and the Allens at the restaurant. After what had happened he hadn't felt like being sociable with anyone, even Marcie, and when she'd come home, accusing him of God knows what, he'd almost lost it. The temptation to tell her that the world didn't revolve about her selfish little life had trembled on the tip of his tongue, and he'd known he had to get out of there before he said—or did—something he'd regret.

And he did regret it this morning, he told himself grimly. He'd been more than generous with Isobel over the years, and he had no reason to feel guilty because she'd chosen to keep her daughter in the dark. What had Emily said? That she was almost eleven? Yes. Definitely old enough to understand that people—even people you loved—didn't always do what was expected of them. He wasn't the traitor here; Isobel was. Emily's mother had betrayed their marriage by having an affair with another man.

Piers Mallory.

His best—*ex*-best—friend.

And she was the result.

He was concentrating so hard on the display he'd brought up on the computer screen that he wasn't aware he was no longer alone. When a hand descended on his shoulder he swore violently, turning a savage face to the intruder.

Shane Harper, his second-in-command, lifted both hands in mock surrender.

'Hey, the door was open,' he said, strolling round Jake's desk. 'I didn't mean to startle you.' He paused, evidently hoping for vindication. 'You're early. Couldn't you sleep?'

'Something like that.' Jake's mouth flattened into a rueful grin. 'Sorry for the profanity. I was miles away.'

'In some dark chasm, by the sound of it,' remarked Shane drily. 'I've got coffee in my room. Want some?'

Jake pushed back his chair from the desk and got to his feet. 'Yeah,' he said, raking back his hair with a careless hand. 'That sounds good. Lead me to it.'

Shane's office, like Jake's and those of the other senior members of staff, opened onto a huge room where many of the other employees worked. Wooden screens divided the floor into booths that gave a semblance of privacy to their occupants. Already one or two operators were at their desks, computer screens flickering to life, eyes blinking owlishly over the mugs of coffee that seemed a necessary jump-start to the day.

Jake followed Shane into an office very like his own and leaned against the door to close it. Then he sprawled into a chair across the desk from Shane's, licking his lips in anticipation when the other man put a mug of steaming black liquid into his hand.

As expected, the coffee was rich and aromatic, the caffeine exactly what he needed to jump-start his own day. It bore no resemblance whatsoever to the instant variety Emily had served him the night before, and he felt a renewed surge of irritation at the thought of Isobel telling her daughter they couldn't afford any better.

That was a lie, pure and simple. The allowance he made his wife, plus what she earned herself, should keep them in relative luxury. But there was no denying that the apartment was beginning to look shabby, and Emily wasn't likely to lie about something like that. So where was the money going? What was she spending it on?

'Hello? Earth to McCabe? Did you just bail out on me again?'

Shane's words brought him out of the deepening depression he'd been sinking into, and Jake pulled a wry face as he took another swallow of his coffee.

'Sorry,' he muttered, trying to concentrate on what was happening in the present instead of drifting back into the past. 'Lack of sleep, I guess. What were you saying?'

'I asked if you'd enjoyed your evening at L'Aiguille,' declared Shane good-naturedly. 'You obviously had a hell of an evening, but I don't know if it was good or bad.'

Jake grunted. 'It wasn't good,' he said, setting the mug down on the desk and rubbing his palms over his knees. 'I didn't get to L'Aiguille.' He grimaced. 'Marcie wasn't pleased.'

'I can believe it.' Shane arched disbelieving brows. 'What happened? I thought you'd arranged to have dinner with the Allens.'

'We had. Marcie did.' Jake lifted his hands and folded them at the back of his neck. 'I didn't.'

Shane frowned. 'I don't understand.'

'No. Nor did she,' remarked Jake with a prolonged sigh. 'It's a long story.'

'Hey.' Shane stared at him. 'Weren't you planning on seeing Isobel yesterday?' A dawning light entered his eyes. 'I get it. Marcie didn't want you to see Isobel. She kicked up a fuss and you bailed out.'

'Yeah.' Jake gave him an old-fashioned look. 'Something like that.'

'But—' Shane would have pursued it further, but a sudden hardening of Jake's expression warned him it would not be wise. Instead, he changed his words. 'How is Isobel, anyway? And that kid of hers? What was her name? Emma?'

'Emily,' Jake amended, before he could stop himself.

Then, dropping his hands, he reached for his coffee again. 'They're fine. Thanks for asking.'

Now it was Shane's turn to give his friend a conservative stare. He'd obviously realised there was more to this than a simple tiff over Jake's wife, but he knew better than to push his luck.

'Great,' he said, reaching for a printout that was lying on his desk. 'By the way, these are the projected figures for Merlin's Mountain. Jay thinks it should supersede all the other games if the results of the ad campaign are anything to go by, and they usually are. Oh, and Steve wants to talk to you about his firewall. According to him, it's the only hacker-proof system there is.'

'And he should know,' observed Jake drily, relieved that the conversation had turned to business matters. He didn't want to offend Shane. They'd been friends too long for him to take the other man's support for granted. But talking about Isobel had never been easy for him and, after last night, he would prefer to be able to put the whole sorry affair out of his mind.

Which wasn't going to happen. He knew that. Knew it even more forcibly later that morning, when his cellphone rang and the small screen displayed Marcie's number.

He was in the middle of a meeting with the finance department at the time, and he was tempted to turn off the phone and ignore it. He could always say he'd left the phone in his office and someone else had hijacked the call. Or he could simply tell her he was busy and that he'd have to call her back.

Some choice.

Stifling a curse, he offered a word of apology to his colleagues and, getting up from the table, crossed to the windows. Standing looking down at the rain-soaked London streets some twenty floors below, he thought how much he hated the city sometimes. He put the phone to his ear. 'McCabe.'

'Jake.'

Marcie's tone was considerably warmer than it had been the night before. Evidently time had mellowed her mood and she was apparently prepared to be magnanimous.

'Marcie.' Despite the overture, Jake felt unaccountably reluctant to return it. 'What can I do for you?'

'So formal, darling.' Marcie's voice would have melted honey. 'Actually, I thought you might have rung me. You know how upset I was last night. I've hardly slept.'

Jake refrained from mentioning that he hadn't been to bed himself. He refused to give her that satisfaction. Instead he said flatly, 'I was pretty bugged myself.'

A silence, and then Marcie spoke again. 'I hope you don't expect me to apologise. Must I remind you that it wasn't me who let you down? What you did was—well, pretty unforgivable. I was made to look like a complete idiot.'

'How?'

Jake heard the accusation in his voice but couldn't seem to help it. Right now he wasn't in the mood for one of Marcie's famous fits of histrionics. Last night he would have told her what had happened, would have explained about Isobel and Emily—well, some of it anyway. Enough to make her realise that he'd had no choice but to do what he had, that on this occasion Isobel had had to come first. But at this moment he didn't much care what she believed.

'You know I wanted you to sound Frank out about the chances of me getting my own show,' Marcie answered, a predictable tremor in her voice. 'You knew I couldn't bring it up myself. I hardly know the Allens. They're your friends, not mine.' She paused, and when he didn't say anything she went on more aggressively, 'And his wife is such a snob. When I told her what I'd been doing for the past five years her jaw almost dropped through the floor. Supercilious bitch! She made me feel like I was the lowest form of pond life. Like she'd never taken her clothes off to get what she wanted. I tell you, Jake, I've had it with women like her. I don't think they know what century they're living in. How I stopped myself from pushing her stupid face into the salmon mousse I'll never know.'

Jake had to smile then. The image of Marcie using strongarm tactics on Virginia Allen was just so ludicrous. Frank's wife was a lady. Heavens, there'd been occasions when she'd refused to attend one of her husband's openings because she'd considered it too risqué. He could quite believe she'd been horrified at the news that Marcie had made her living as a photographic model. In her opinion, models—fashion models included—were not much better than paid courtesans.

'I'd like to have seen that,' he said now, the humour in his voice unmistakable, and Marcie giggled.

'You might have, if you'd been there,' she said tartly, proving that she hadn't quite forgiven him yet. Then, evidently deciding she ought to quit while she was ahead, she added, 'So how about joining me for lunch instead? I've got some champagne in the fridge I'd intended to open last night. We could see what novel ways we can find to drink it. What do you say, darling? It's Louis Roederer. Your favourite.'

It was a tempting offer, but Jake had to refuse it. 'I can't,' he said. 'I'm meeting a supplier for lunch, and this afternoon I'm flying to Brussels to meet up with our European distributors. I don't expect I'll be back much before midnight.'

Marcie groaned. Then, with obvious inspiration, 'I could come with you. I'm free all day.'

'I don't think so.' Jake let her down lightly. 'How much work do you think I'd get done with you along for the ride?

No, Marcie. I guess we're going to have to put the champagne on ice for another day.'

'If I don't find someone else to drink it with, you mean?' she flashed shortly, and Jake expelled a weary breath.

'Your call,' he said drily, aware that a significant silence had fallen behind him. He'd been on the phone too long, and there was only so much that could be decided in his absence.

'So I won't see you until Saturday,' Marcie said tightly.

'Looks that way,' agreed Jake, casting an apologetic glance over his shoulder. 'I'll call you when I get back.'

The sound of Marcie's phone disconnecting was his answer, and he pulled a face at his reflection in the rain-washed windows before closing his own phone and slipping it into his pocket.

Then he turned back to his colleagues. 'Sorry about that, gentlemen,' he said, forcing a smile for their benefit. 'What's that expression? A little local difficulty, right? Now, where were we?'

Isobel was tempted to keep Emily home from school the next morning. The girl had had a restless night, crying out in her sleep, waking herself up every couple of hours to go to the bathroom. Naturally Isobel hadn't slept much either, and they were both hollow-eyed at breakfast.

But she had a pile of properties on her desk at work, and meetings with clients scheduled for most of the morning. Isobel knew she didn't dare take another day off. She'd already stretched her boss's goodwill to breaking point in looking after her mother, and she didn't kid herself that her skill at selling houses was indispensable.

Besides, she had the feeling that her daughter would be better off at school. Staying at home would only remind her of what had happened the night before, and Isobel was desperate that Emily should put that unpleasantness behind her. She was only a child, after all. She didn't understand. Jake should never have taken out his own frustration with Isobel on the girl.

Yet what had she expected? She'd known that sooner or later he—or someone else—would tell Emily of the doubts concerning her paternity. Her mother had threatened to do so more than once. But Isobel had warned her, on pain of excommunication, not to say anything to upset the child until she was old enough to handle it.

And they'd been getting along with their lives quite well. They weren't well off. Emily's school fees, and the money Isobel paid towards her mother's expenses, ensured that there was little change at the end of the month. But she knew there were others far less comfortable than themselves.

Lady Hannah's illness, however, had made a severe dent in her income—and her confidence. Isobel had had no idea where she would find the money to pay for her mother's treatment. The idea of the old lady having to wait to have her operation in a National Health hospital had not been an option. The doctor had admitted that Lady Hannah might die before the life-saving surgery was performed, and there'd been no way Isobel could allow that to happen.

She suspected Jake might have loaned her the money if she'd asked him. But she'd had no desire to involve him, no desire to precipitate exactly what had happened the night before. So she'd sold her car, and what little jewellery she'd possessed, and cut their expenses to the bone to pay back the mortgage she'd raised on the apartment.

Of course, she hadn't anticipated that Jake might want to see her, that her mother might be taken ill on the very afternoon he was due to arrive. It was years since there'd been any serious contact between them. If he needed to speak to her, he usually phoned, and she'd actually begun to believe that Emily might be a young woman before

Isobel had to confess her part in Jake's estrangement from his family.

But that was before Marcie Duncan came on the scene. Marcie, who was young and beautiful, who didn't just want an affair, who wanted a husband.

Isobel's husband.

'Am I really not—not *his* daughter?' Emily asked suddenly, as Isobel was wondering what she was going to tell her mother when she visited her this evening, and she turned to look at the child. She'd been so wrapped up in her own thoughts she hadn't noticed that Emily had put down her cereal spoon and was regarding her now with wide, troubled eyes.

'No, you are his daughter.' Isobel was adamant. She didn't care if she aggravated Jake; she wasn't going to lie to the child. 'We talked about this last night, Em, and I told you not to worry about it. Whatever—Daddy—says, however painful his words may be, you are his daughter. You're *our* daughter. And—I love you very much.'

'He doesn't.' Emily was dogged, and she pushed her untouched bowl aside. Then, cautiously, 'Why doesn't he believe us?'

Isobel stifled a groan. 'I—your father has never forgiven me for something I did before you were born,' she admitted at last. 'It's my fault, not his.'

Emily frowned. 'What did you do?'

But that was beyond even Isobel's abilities to explain. 'It's not important now,' she said, getting up from the breakfast bar and carrying her coffee cup to the sink. 'Go on, eat your cornflakes. We've got to leave in ten minutes and I want to phone the hospital first.'

'The hospital?' To Isobel's relief, Emily was distracted, and although she didn't make any attempt to eat her cereal, she was obviously concerned. 'How long is Granny going to be in hospital?'

'I don't know.' Anxiety clogged Isobel's throat for a moment. Although the events of the night before had served to divert her thoughts from her mother's relapse, the reality of the situation was suddenly almost too much to bear. She and Lady Hannah hadn't always seen eye-to-eye, and there'd been times when Isobel had thought the old lady was going out of her way to cause trouble for her. But she was her mother, her only living relative apart from Emily, and if anything happened to her she'd be completely devastated. On top of everything else it just seemed too much.

'Is she going to die?'

Emily's voice betrayed the panic that Isobel was trying so hard to hide, and in an effort to reassure the child she gave a short laugh.

'Of course not!' she exclaimed, pointing at Emily's dish again. 'You can come with me to see her this evening. Now, eat your breakfast. I don't want you falling ill, too.'

To her relief, Emily picked up her spoon and made a gallant attempt to swallow her cereal. But she was still upset, and Isobel wondered again if she ought to send her to school in this state.

But she didn't have a lot of choice. Without her mother to call on she was severely limited in the arrangements she could make. There was always Sarah Daniels, of course, but although her friend had always professed herself willing to act as babysitter, she had three children of her own to care for.

Thankfully it was a fine morning, and Isobel and Emily were able to walk the quarter-mile to the Lady Stafford School, where Emily was in her third year. In another couple of years, she'd have to transfer to the upper school, and Isobel dreaded to think what the fees would be then. But for the moment she was coping, and she refused to worry about something that was so far in the future when the present was so abominably uncertain.

Isobel saw Emily into her classroom, and then went to speak to Mrs Reynolds, the head teacher. She explained that her mother had been taken ill again and that Emily was naturally very upset about it.

It wasn't the whole truth, but it was sufficiently convincing for Mrs Reynolds to assure her that she'd have a word with Emily's teacher and ask her to be especially vigilant with the child today.

'Girls of that age can be overly anxious about these matters,' she said, patting Isobel's arm as she accompanied her to the door of her office. 'I'm sure she'll be all right. And do give Lady Hannah our best wishes for a speedy recovery, won't you?'

Isobel said she would, but as she left the school she couldn't help taking a fleeting look up at Emily's classroom. It didn't reassure her to see her daughter standing at the window, watching her departure, and she continued on her way to work with a heavy heart.

CHAPTER FOUR

JAKE was trying to get his briefcase to close when his secretary came to stand in the open doorway to his office.

'Pete's just phoned to say you've got a visitor on her way up,' she said, her lips twitching with what Jake suspected was wry humour, and he closed his eyes for a moment, wishing he'd left fifteen minutes ago.

He had no doubts that he knew who it was. Since the phone call earlier he'd been half expecting Marcie to try to get in touch with him again, and it appeared he'd been right.

'I assume Pete told her I was still here?' he said, wondering why he hadn't thought to warn the commissionaire that he didn't have time to see any visitors, however tenacious they might be.

Lucy Givens smiled. 'Why wouldn't he?' she asked. 'You can hardly refuse to see her, can you?'

Jake scowled. 'I could,' he said, but he knew he wouldn't. 'I don't suppose you—?'

'Hey, I don't even know her,' said Lucy, raising both hands in a gesture of denial, and Jake sighed.

'Where is she?'

'Like I said, she's on her way up,' said Lucy, with the familiarity of fifteen years experience. 'Good luck!'

Jake thought that was a little too close to the bone, even for Lucy, but she had already turned back into her cubicle. He dropped his briefcase onto his desk before following her.

And was just in time to see the small figure who exited from the lift.

'My God! It's Emily,' he said, looking down at Lucy, who had resumed her seat at her desk, with incredulous eyes. 'Did you know?'

'Pete said she'd said she was your daughter,' admitted Lucy, getting up to scan the girl who was hovering uncertainly at the end of the room. 'My God, she's just a kid!'

'What did you expect?' exclaimed Jake, raking his nails over his scalp in sudden frustration. 'Dammit, I'm not that old!'

Lucy arched considering brows. 'I guess not,' she conceded. 'I must say, you've kept her identity a secret.'

Jake's jaw compressed. The words *She's not my daughter* stuck in his throat, but he couldn't get them out. Not now. Not with Emily suddenly catching sight of him and heading purposefully in his direction. He couldn't do that to her, to himself. For the moment he had to let it stand and, suppressing an oath, he went to meet her.

'Hi,' she said, a little nervously, and for the first time he wondered how she'd got here, how she'd known where to find him. Surely Isobel hadn't told her, hadn't sent her? Not after what had happened the night before.

'Hi,' he said in return and, realising they were attracting far too much attention from the rest of his staff, gestured behind him. 'D'you want to come into my office?'

'Mmm—yes, please.'

Emily was remarkably eager, and Jake thought how different she was this afternoon from the way she'd behaved the previous day. Had something happened? he wondered. Had Isobel explained why they were no longer together?

Lucy smiled at the girl as they passed her desk, and Jake was forced to introduce them. 'Um, this is my secretary, Lucy Givens,' he said awkwardly. 'Lucy, this is Emily—'

'McCabe,' finished the girl proudly. 'Emily McCabe.' She held out her hand. 'How do you do? I'm pleased to meet you.'

'Likewise,' murmured Lucy, with a covert glance at her employer. 'Is this your first visit to the office, Emily?'

'Yes.' Emily was amazingly self-composed, considering the circumstances, and Jake realised he'd been too ambitious in thinking Isobel might have told her the truth. 'But it's nice, isn't it? And big. Really big!'

'We like it.'

Lucy pulled a wry face at Jake and, deciding it was time to end this exchange, he ushered Emily ahead of him into the large corner office he occupied.

Then, glancing over his shoulder, he said, 'You'd better call Howard and tell him I won't be needing the helicopter for another—' he consulted his watch '—for another half-hour at least.'

'Okay.'

Lucy spoke demurely enough, but he could tell she was enjoying his discomfort. It wasn't every day she had something so juicy to gossip about, and the arrival of a hitherto unknown daughter was certainly that.

He was tempted to tell her to keep her mouth shut, but it would have been a wasted effort. Emily's arrival had been noticed by too many people for him to even imagine he could keep it a secret. Consequently, he was feeling justifiably harried when he closed the door and found Emily looking round his office with a decidedly proprietary air. She was still wearing her school uniform, but she'd dropped her haversack onto the floor. She evidently felt she had a right to be there, and his initial reaction was to swiftly disabuse her of that belief.

But then she turned to look at him, her eyes suspiciously bright and swimming with unshed tears, and his resentment faltered. However confident she'd seemed in front of Lucy, coming here had evidently taken a lot of guts, and she was having a struggle now in holding on to her composure.

'You—you don't mind me coming, do you?' she asked

unsteadily, and Jake found he hadn't the heart to be angry with her.

'I—does your mother know where you are?' he said instead, avoiding a direct answer, and she sighed.

'No.'

Jake frowned. 'Then won't she be worried about you?'

'Not yet.' Emily moved to look out of the windows. 'We're very high up, aren't we?'

'Twenty floors,' agreed Jake. 'But you know that. You came up in the lift.'

'Yes.' Emily seemed to realise something more was expected of her and she turned round again. 'Mummy won't miss me until she gets home from work.'

'Which is when?'

'Five o'clock.' Emily shrugged. 'Or thereabouts. Sometimes she's early; sometimes she's late.'

'How late?'

'Half-past five. It was six o'clock once, but that was because a client was late getting to the property.'

Jake could feel himself getting annoyed again. But not with Emily this time. Dear heaven, didn't Isobel know Emily was too young to be a latchkey kid? Why the hell didn't she employ a childminder for a couple of hours in the afternoon? A neighbour would do. Just someone to make sure Emily didn't get into mischief in her absence.

Like coming here!

'Okay,' he said, realising this was something he would have to take up with Isobel. He indicated a grouping of armchairs and a low-backed sofa in the corner. 'Why don't you sit down and tell me why you've come?'

Emily hesitated. 'I think you know why I've come,' she said, making no attempt to do as he'd suggested. 'I want to talk to you about Mummy.'

Jake's eyes widened. Mummy! Yeah, right.

'Go on,' he said, moving to the desk and propping his

hips against the polished granite. 'What about your mother?'

Emily bit her lip. Then, wrapping her arms about her midriff, she said quickly, 'I know why you're not together any more.'

Jake's brows descended. 'You do?' he said, trying not to show his astonishment, and Emily nodded.

'Yes. She told me. She said she'd done something—I suppose it must have been really bad—and you wouldn't forgive her.' She licked her lips. 'But she's sorry; I know she is. Mummy doesn't do things to hurt people. You ask Granny.'

Jake's shoulders sagged. 'And that's why you came all this way?'

'Mmm.' Emily's eyes were still too bright, but there was a definite hint of expectation in her expression. She sniffed, rubbing her nose with a nervous finger. 'I wanted to ask you to forgive her. For me.' She took a beat. 'I want us to be a family again.'

Bloody hell!

Jake wondered if he was being naïve in thinking Isobel hadn't put this idea into her head. Emily was ten years old, for pity's sake. How the hell had she known where to find him if her mother hadn't told her? And how had she got here? Emily's school was on the other side of town.

'Look,' he said, desperately searching for a way to salvage this. 'I don't—that is—' Her eyes, those luminous blue eyes, gazed into his and he was defeated. 'What— how—how did you know where I worked?' he finished lamely, and Emily's smile briefly appeared.

'I looked you up in the telephone directory at school,' she said proudly. 'McCabe Tectonics. That's what you call your company, don't you? It was easy to find.'

Jake blew out a breath. 'And how did you get here? Did you take a cab?'

'A cab?' Emily looked puzzled for a moment. 'Oh, you mean a mini-cab,' she said, understanding. 'Heavens, no. I couldn't afford a mini-cab. I caught a bus.'

'A bus!' Despite his affirmation that Emily was not his daughter—and therefore not his responsibility—Jake was horrified. The idea of her leaving school and catching a bus across town was bad enough, but no one had known what she intended to do. No one had known where she was going. And if, by some means Jake didn't even want to contemplate, she'd disappeared, no one would have been any the wiser.

'It's all right,' Emily assured him, evidently picking up on his consternation. 'I catch the bus home from school every afternoon.'

'And that's what? Three stops?' Jake's voice was curt, but he couldn't help it. 'Dammit, Emily, you don't go traipsing around town without telling anyone what you're doing. What if you'd been—?' He broke off, amending his words. 'What if you'd been—kidnapped?'

'Because I'm your daughter, you mean?'

Emily was evidently considering this and, losing patience with both himself and her, Jake pushed away from the desk and strode towards the door.

Yanking it open, he confronted a startled Lucy, who was talking on the phone. She hung up at once, however, adding to his sense of frustration, and his tone lacked any of its usual humour when he said, 'Cancel my trip to Brussels, will you? Get onto Helmut Leitnich and offer him my apologies. Tell him we'll have to reschedule the meeting for next week.'

Lucy, whose face was a little pink now, nodded energetically. 'Yes, Jake.'

'Oh, and tell Pete I'll need my car in about fifteen minutes. After you've brought us coffee and orange juice—right?'

Lucy got to her feet. 'Coffee and orange juice,' she echoed. 'Got it.'

'Good.' Jake paused. And then, because he refused to let her think that *she* was making a fool of him, too, he added brusquely, 'And if I find out you've been prattling about this to all and sundry, you'd better start looking for another job!'

Isobel saw the sleek black Porsche parked a few yards down from number twenty-three as she walked home.

She was tired, and anxious, and she wouldn't have noticed the car at all if it hadn't looked so familiar. It was similar to Jake's car, and she wondered which of her neighbours had fallen in love with it. It looked in excellent condition. Its paintwork was immaculate, its alloy wheels gleaming like new. Even its number plate was—the same!

And that was when she started to panic.

She ran the last few yards to her gate, fumbling in her bag for her keys as she went up the steps to the front door. But the door opened as she reached it, proving that someone had been watching for her approach. She took the stairs more quickly than she would have thought possible in her present depressed condition.

All thoughts about her mother, about what the doctor had told her when she'd rushed to the hospital in her lunch hour, were forgotten as she reached her door. What was Jake doing here? What had he been saying to Emily? Had he decided to endorse last night's revelations with a more precise version of her shortcomings? To prove to the child once and for all that he wanted no part of her, of either of them?

Emily opened the door before she could use her key, but there was no sign of any distress in her expression. On the contrary, Isobel thought she looked a little guilty, as if she'd been doing something she shouldn't. And for the first

time Isobel wondered if Jake's car being in the street outside might just be a coincidence.

It didn't last long. 'Daddy's here,' Emily announced,
with what sounded like unnecessary haste. 'He brought me
home.'

'He did?'

Isobel was confused. She moved into the hall, allowing
the door to close behind her, unbuttoning her coat with
fingers that were not quite steady.

'You'd better tell your mother where I brought you home
from,' remarked Jake laconically, coming to prop his shoulder against the drawing room doorway, and Isobel looked
up to find her husband regarding her with enigmatic eyes.

'Where you brought her home from?' she echoed
blankly, dropping her coat onto the chest that stood beneath
an antique mirror and turning to look at her daughter again.
'I don't understand—'

Emily hunched her shoulders. 'He brought me home
from the office,' she said with sulky emphasis, and Isobel's
eyes widened in dismay.

'You—you went to—to his office?' she asked, realising
that although she'd thought things couldn't get any worse
they already had. 'Oh, Em…'

'It's no big deal,' muttered Emily. 'Why shouldn't I go
to his office? Other girls do.'

'I don't care what other girls do,' said Isobel, dreading
to think what Jake must have thought. 'Oh, Em, don't you
think I have enough to worry about without you creating
more problems?'

'What problems?'

Jake had straightened away from the door, and now
Isobel permitted herself to look his way. Until then she'd
barely noticed what he was wearing, but now she saw how
formally dressed he was. The narrow trousers of his char-
coal suit outlined the powerful length of his legs, and be-

neath the double-breasted jacket a black turtleneck sweater was his concession to a shirt.

As always, he looked dangerously good to her, and she made a play of replacing her keys in her handbag to give herself time to construct her answer. 'Oh—you know,' she said, wishing he would move out of the doorway and give her a little space. 'This and that.'

'Granny's in hospital again,' put in Emily, evidently eager to say anything to divert their attention from her misdoings, and Jake's brows descended.

'She is?' he said, looking at Isobel through lashes that were absurdly long for a man. 'You didn't tell me that.'

'When have I had the chance to tell you anything?' Isobel countered and, growing tired of the impasse, eased her way past him to head down the hall.

As she'd half expected he followed her, with Emily not far behind. 'This is why you were so late last night,' he said flatly. 'I should have asked.'

'It's not your problem,' replied Isobel, tossing her handbag onto the counter and checking that the kettle was full. 'How long have you been here?'

'Not long.' Jake glanced behind him. 'Why don't you go and do your homework, Emily?' he suggested, his tone denying any argument. 'I need to speak to your mother.'

'But—'

'Privately,' he added warningly. 'I think you've pushed your luck far enough for one day, don't you?'

Emily pursed her lips. 'You will tell me when you're leaving, won't you? So I can say goodbye?'

Jake heaved a sigh. 'If you like.'

'Okay.'

Emily grinned and lifted her hand, and almost automatically, it seemed, she and Jake exchanged a high five. Then, with an appealing look at her mother, she scooted off to her bedroom, and Isobel and Jake were left alone.

'I'm sorry,' Isobel said at once, wondering if she would ever be in a position where she didn't have to apologise to this man. 'I had no idea Em might—that is, she had no right to come to your office. I hope she didn't cause a problem for you.'

'Yeah, right.' Jake was sardonic, but unlike the night before he didn't exploit his advantage. 'Hey, they're all wondering where I've been keeping my daughter all these years. No sweat!'

Isobel's lips parted. 'You told them she was your daughter?' she asked in an awed voice, and Jake's mouth thinned.

'I didn't tell them anything,' he corrected her drily. 'I didn't have to.' Then, when she turned back to fumble with the tea caddy, he added, 'How is the old girl, anyway? Still calling down the hounds of Hades on my head, right? Funny, I'd have thought she'd break out the Jack Daniels when we split up. But she still puts the knife in any chance she gets.'

Isobel turned to look at him, her brows drawing together. 'You still see her?'

'From time to time,' agreed Jake, lifting a dismissive shoulder. 'When she needs some repairs to that old ruin she calls her home.'

Isobel was stunned. 'She never said a word to me.'

'Why would she?' Jake shrugged. 'It suits her very well to keep you and me apart. I think she's afraid I might forgive you for sleeping with Mallory. She puts up with me bankrolling her, but she wouldn't like to see us get back together.'

Isobel's fingers trembled as she lifted the kettle. 'I don't believe it,' she said, her hand shaking so much that she splashed hot water over her wrist. 'Oh, damn,' she mumbled, the pain of the scalding water on top of everything else bringing tears to her eyes. 'She wouldn't do that. Not without telling me. She—she has too much pride.'

'Pride's a pretty cold bedfellow if your house is falling down about your ears,' retorted Jake, striding across the room and taking the kettle out of her hand. Then, grasping her arm, he turned on the cold tap and held her burning wrist under its spray. 'Don't worry, Belle. I can afford it. It's a small price to pay to keep that old harridan off my back.'

Isobel quivered. It was a long time since he'd touched her, since she had been this close to him, her senses assaulted by his distinctive smell. It mingled with the lingering fragrance of the aftershave he'd used that morning, the clean male scent of his body overlaid by a heated trace of sweat that was evident when the sides of his jacket moved apart.

It was all so intimate, so familiar, and she longed to turn into him and press her hot face against his chest.

She remembered distinctly how he would feel, how the taut muscles of his stomach would tighten against her midriff. She could feel her breasts pebbling now, in anticipation of his nearness, feel the liquid heat of her own arousal throbbing like a pulse between her legs.

Dear God, it was madness, but she still wanted him, wanted to feel his arms around her, holding her, supporting her, comforting her...

Yes, that was it, she told herself fiercely, latching onto anything to save her crumbling self-respect. After the day she'd had, after the things she'd learned about her mother, she was desperate for any comfort, any affection. She felt so alone, so helpless in the face of her mother's illness, so vulnerable against the demands she continued to make, that she was ready to welcome any overture, however innocent it might be.

But she made the mistake of looking up at him, and whatever Jake saw in her face was enough to alert him to the dangers of the situation. 'Just keep it under the water for a few more seconds,' he said stiffly, his words so prosaic and practical that for a moment she found it difficult to comprehend what he was saying. But he'd dropped her arm and moved back from her, and she was instantly aware of what she had done.

And despised herself anew for letting him see how pathetically needful she was.

Turning off the tap, she grabbed a kitchen towel from the roll and blotted her wrist. The skin had reddened, but it was much easier now, and after resetting the kettle on its hob she forced herself to face him.

'Thanks,' she said, her voice equally as neutral as his. 'I'll have to take more care in future.'

'Yeah.' And, as if Jake had decided to take his cue from her, he added, 'Are you all right? You got quite a shock there.'

'I've been scalded before,' she said, taking mugs from the shelf. 'Do you want some tea?'

Jake hesitated, and she could almost see him mentally glancing at his watch. 'Whatever,' he said at last, apparently deciding he had something more to say. 'So how is the old girl? You never did get around to telling me.'

Isobel concentrated on taking teabags from the box. 'She's—dying, actually,' she said offhandedly, unable to handle it any other way. 'I forget—do you take milk and sugar?'

Jake's oath overrode her enquiry, and the teabags scattered as he grasped her by the shoulders and swung her round to face him. 'She's *what*?'

Isobel couldn't look at him. Not now, when she was so close to the edge. 'I think you heard what I said,' she said, once again compelled to confront her weakness where he was concerned. She glanced about her. 'I must pick up the teabags—'

'To hell with the teabags,' muttered Jake savagely, his

hands on her shoulders flexing with the agitation in his voice. 'Dammit, Belle, why didn't you tell me it was this serious? I thought the operation had been a success.'

'So did we,' Isobel admitted, making a concerted effort to break free. 'Jake, the kettle's boiling. If you don't let me go it's going to fill the place with steam.'

Jake looked down at her half impatiently. She was aware of his eyes upon her, aware that this time there was more than frustration in his stare. But she didn't make the mistake of meeting his gaze, however easy it would have been to take advantage of his sympathy. If he comforted her now it would be a mechanical thing, at best, and she couldn't bear to be the recipient of such dispassionate emotion.

'Jake,' she said again, lifting her hands and pressing him away from her, and this time he seemed to realise that she might misinterpret his actions.

'Yeah, yeah,' he said, opening his fingers and letting her move out of his grasp. But she noticed that his hands balled into fists before falling to his sides, and she realised that learning of her mother's imminent demise had been a shock to him, too.

However, he pulled himself together sufficiently to help her gather up the teabags from the floor, and when their eyes accidentally met he didn't immediately look away. Instead, for the minutest space of time, she glimpsed something much darker than sympathy in his gaze and her breathing quickened to a laboured gasp.

Then he swung away, dropping the teabags he'd collected on the counter and walking almost reflexively towards the door. She guessed he wanted to go, to get out of there before he said or did something he'd regret. But something—some desire to satisfy himself that she hadn't been lying to him, perhaps—caused him to stop and turn back.

'So what's the prognosis?' he asked shortly. 'How long have you known?'

'I just found out today,' replied Isobel, keeping her voice steady with an effort. She lifted the kettle and filled the pot before continuing doggedly, 'It appears there has been a serious deterioration in her condition. It can happen. The doctor believes the disease has spread to the arteries. In layman's terms, she's suffering from heart failure.'

'Heart failure?' Jake shook his head. 'Isn't that what happens when you have a heart attack?'

'Apparently not.' Isobel moistened her lips. 'Heart attacks are caused by a blockage of the arteries. Heart failure, as the name implies, takes much longer. Weeks, maybe even months.'

Jake blew out a breath. 'And does she know?'

'I think so.'

'You think so?' Jake stared at her. 'Surely you didn't—?'

'No one's actually told her she's dying,' exclaimed Isobel fiercely. 'What do you think we are? Heartless?' She pulled a face at the involuntary pun and then made an impatient gesture. 'You know Lady Hannah. She's not stupid. She knows something's wrong. That's why she wants—'

She broke off then, aware that she was in danger of confiding in a man to whom her mother's failing health could only be a bonus. If he had been giving her money it would doubtless be a relief to be free of that responsibility.

But Jake was waiting for her to go on and, forcing a faint smile, she said, 'Let's just say that's why she's already started making demands.'

'What demands?'

Jake's immediate response didn't give her time to think of a convincing explanation. 'This and that,' she said, hoping he'd take the hint and not pursue it. 'Um—shall we go into the living room?'

'What demands?' asked Jake again, and although Isobel had been about to pick up the tray, she wrapped her arms about herself instead.

She could feel the chilliness of her skin beneath the thin material of her blouse, but she knew it wasn't just the coolness of the apartment that was to blame. 'Do you care?' she demanded at last, when it seemed obvious he was determined to have an answer. 'Our affairs are nothing to do with you. You've told me so I don't know how many times.'

'Isobel!'

'Oh—all right.' With a sigh, she gave in. 'She wants to go back to Yorkshire.'

'You're kidding!' Jake was stunned. 'But she hasn't lived there for years. Not since—not since—'

'Just after we split up?' Isobel finished tightly. 'I know that. Nevertheless, she has always considered Mattingley her real home.' She pulled a wry face. 'She even insisted on Emily being born there.'

'Yeah.' Jake spoke grimly. 'Well— But dammit, Belle, the place has to be rundown, and damp. Hell, it's only six months since she was telling me the roof was leaking. She can't stay there now.'

Isobel lifted her shoulders. 'Do you want to tell her that?'

Jake stifled an oath. 'She's crazy.'

'No. Just old,' said Isobel softly. 'And afraid of the future. Perhaps she thinks she might get better at Mattingley. Whatever, somehow I'm going to take her there. It's the least I can do.'

Jake raked impatient fingers through his hair. 'You're going to take a sick woman to a practically derelict property? Get real, Belle. Do you have any idea how much work will be entailed? Apart from anything else it will need a thorough clean-out.'

Isobel held up her head. 'The Edwardses still live there,'

she said with dignity. 'They'll have kept it in reasonable order.'

'The Edwardses were old when we got married,' retorted Jake roughly. 'Okay, they may have ensured that any necessary repairs were reported, and that the place didn't get infested with bugs or other vermin. But Mattingley is too big for two people to cope with—particularly two people who must be in their eighties by now.'

'Their seventies, actually,' said Isobel stiffly, aware that he was only voicing her own fears and resenting him because of it. 'We'll manage.'

Jake stared at her. 'What about this place? What about your job?' He paused. 'What about Emily's schooling?'

Isobel gave him a cynical look. 'Like you care.'

Jake's fists clenched. 'Okay,' he said harshly, and she knew she had gone too far. 'Do what you like.' He paused, and then added coldly, 'And keep that kid the hell away from my office, right?'

CHAPTER FIVE

LUCY had rescheduled Jake's trip to Brussels for Tuesday. As well as meeting his European supplier, he also wanted to see the minister involved, and he couldn't make it on Monday.

Which was just as well, Jake thought, when he arrived at work on Monday morning. After the weekend he'd had he was in no mood to conduct delicate negotiations, and the bottle of single malt he'd downed before going to bed had left his head feeling as thick as a plank with nails that bored into his skull.

Thankfully, Lucy wasn't yet at her desk, and Jake was able to make the comparative sanctuary of his office without incident. He knew he looked like hell. He hadn't shaved before he left home, and the V-necked sweatshirt he was wearing under a leather jacket was the same one he'd been wearing the day before.

He slumped into the chair behind his desk, wishing he'd picked up a cup of coffee from the machine before he'd holed up here. Several shots of caffeine might make his brain feel clearer, but he doubted it. The way he felt right now, nothing but time would cure him of his hangover.

The phone, with its sophisticated call-system, mocked him. Marcie would be expecting him to call, he knew, but he still didn't know what he was going to say to her. He knew what she wanted him to say, what she *expected* him to say, but it wasn't that easy.

How could he expect Isobel to cope with their divorce on top of everything else? He couldn't do that to her. And, what was more, he didn't want to hurt her in that way. Not

64

in the present circumstances. Okay, maybe she hadn't always been as scrupulous of his feelings, but he knew how fragile she was right now and he didn't want to be the one to break her.

And he sensed that that would.

Which was why he had spent most of the weekend fighting both Marcie—and his own conscience.

His girlfriend—probably not unreasonably—had been furious when she'd heard about Emily's visit to his office. Despite what he'd told her about Isobel having to come to terms with the fact that her mother was dying, Marcie's main objection had been that the girl had had the nerve to turn up uninvited. She wouldn't accept that Isobel had known nothing about it. She was convinced it was a ploy to persuade him that the child was his, and to embarrass *her*.

Of course, Jake had insisted that it had all been perfectly innocent, that no harm had been done, but Marcie hadn't swallowed that. The fact was Emily had announced herself as his daughter, and in Marcie's eyes that was unforgivable.

And it was. In his more aggressive moments he had to admit she had a point. If Isobel had wanted to embarrass him—embarrass both of them—she couldn't have chosen a better way to do it, and it was only because he knew his wife had spent much of the afternoon at the hospital that he'd accepted she was innocent of any wrongdoing. Besides, he'd known at once that he was the very last person she'd wanted to see when she had let herself into the apartment on Friday evening. Her reaction had proved that.

His mouth compressed. He didn't want to think about it, but it bugged him no end that Isobel looked so tired all the time. Okay, she was having a tough week, what with her mother and all, but he objected to the way she looked at him, as if he was personally responsible for the mess she'd made of her life.

Nevertheless, that didn't alter the fact that the row he'd had with Marcie on Saturday morning was still unresolved. Her complete indifference to the demands of the situation had really got to him, and after what she'd said when he'd explained that he'd had to postpone his trip to Belgium he hadn't even broached the concerns he had about Isobel and Lady Hannah going to live in that derelict old mansion in Yorkshire.

Dammit, he thought, at the very least the place was going to need a thorough spring-cleaning, and he knew, without a shadow of a doubt, that Isobel would be the one to do it...

But that wasn't his problem, he rebuked himself angrily. Why couldn't he accept that, as Marcie had said, it wasn't his concern? After all, she hadn't wanted to believe that Lady Hannah's illness was even genuine.

'It's very convenient,' she'd declared callously. 'The old woman choosing this particular moment to develop a life-threatening condition.'

'I don't think she chose it,' Jake had replied mildly, holding onto his temper with an effort. 'She had open-heart surgery last year. There was nothing convenient about that.'

Marcie's eyes had sparked. 'And you know this because...?'

'Emily told me,' he said flatly.

'Emily!' Marcie's expression had hardened. 'Isobel's little bastard! *She* told you. And, of course, her word is so much more convincing than mine.'

'Don't be so bloody ridiculous!'

Hearing Emily described in those terms once again had pricked a nerve, and Jake had found himself defending the child with more passion than intellect. The upshot was that the argument had deteriorated from that point on and they'd both ended up saying things they didn't necessarily mean. Jake had spent the rest of the weekend regretting the incident—but not enough to pick up the phone and make amends.

But now it was Monday morning, and he knew he would have to do something to heal the breach. He might be feeling sorry for Isobel, he told himself irritably, but it was Marcie he loved. Marcie he was going to marry, as soon as he could get a divorce...

A knock at his door saved him from the perversity of his thoughts. 'Yeah?' he called, hoping it wasn't Lucy, coming to find out what had happened to his 'daughter', and nodded in some relief when Shane Harper poked his head into the room.

'Can I come in?' Shane asked doubtfully, the closed door so unusual he'd felt compelled to ask. 'I've got coffee.'

'Just what I need,' said Jake, getting out of his chair to take the mug his friend was offering. 'Mmm, that's good. Black enough to lead a stove, as my old gran used to say.'

'I didn't know you had an old gran,' remarked Shane drily, lounging onto the sofa by the windows, and Jake pulled a wry face.

'Everybody has an old gran,' he countered, propping his hips against his desk. 'We don't always get to know them, that's all.'

Shane regarded him sceptically. 'And you knew yours?'

'No.' Jake arched mocking brows. 'But it's what she would have said if I had.'

'Yeah, right.' Shane was laconic. 'I'd have said it was just a couple of shades darker than the bags beneath your eyes, pal. What happened to you? You look like hell!'

Jake regarded him from between narrowed lids. 'Thanks.'

'Hey, no sweat!' Shane was on a roll. 'I guess finding out you've got a daughter you didn't know you had can do that to you.'

Jake's brows drew together. 'Don't go there, Harper.'

'Why not?' Shane was defensive now. 'Luce told me she was your daughter. Where's the harm in that?'

Jake scowled. He should have known Lucy would be unable to keep Emily's identity to herself. Besides, Pete Warden, the doorman, had sent her up in the lift. If he knew about it, everybody would. Just because Shane hadn't been around when Emily arrived that didn't mean he wouldn't have heard the gossip.

'She's—Isobel's daughter,' Jake muttered, despising himself for not being more positive. 'I guess she wanted to see where I worked.'

'Right.' Shane looked only a little less apprehensive. He shook his head. 'I didn't even know Isobel had got married again.'

Jake gritted his teeth. 'She hasn't.'

'Then—'

'She had Emily after we split up,' he said flatly, taking a gulp of his coffee and almost scalding his mouth in the process. 'God, this is hot!'

Shane was still looking doubtful, however, and Jake knew he must be wondering what the hell he'd meant. Giving in to a totally selfish desire to exonerate himself, he said, 'Emily's not my daughter.'

Shane blinked. 'So who is her father?'

'I don't know.'

His friend frowned. 'Come on, Jake, you've got to know. Isobel didn't sleep around.'

'How do you know that?'

Shane flushed. 'Well, not through trying,' he said shortly. 'Dammit, Jake, Luce said the kid was at least ten or eleven. How long is it since you and Isobel split up?'

Jake heaved a sigh. 'I don't want to get into this.'

'Why not?' Shane stared at him. 'Hey, you don't think you could have made a mistake?'

'No.'

''Cos you could always find out,' continued Shane blandly. 'DNA tests are pretty foolproof—'

'I don't want to talk about this,' said Jake harshly. He had no intention of discussing Isobel's affair with Shane. 'Drop it, will you?'

'So…' Shane hesitated. 'How did she get home?'

'Who?'

'Emily, of course. Did you take her?'

'What if I did?'

'I'm only asking.' Shane lifted a hand in a gesture of defeat. 'How is the lovely Mrs McCabe anyway?'

'Soon to be *ex*,' retorted Jake grimly. Then, less aggressively, 'She's okay. I think.'

'You think?' Shane seemed to know he was pushing his luck, but he and Jake had been friends too long to allow this affair to spoil their relationship. 'Why the proviso?'

'Because—' Jake broke off and then went on reluctantly, 'She has a lot on her plate at the moment.'

'Like what?'

'Her mother's very ill,' said Jake, taking another gulp of his coffee. 'And she wants to go back to the so-called family seat to die.'

'Oh, right.' Shane nodded. 'She's a Lady, isn't she?'

Jake grimaced. 'That's a matter of opinion. But, yes, she's Lady Hannah Lacey. Isobel was born and brought up at their country house, Mattingley, in Yorkshire.'

'Cool.'

Shane looked impressed, but Jake was quick to correct him. 'Not cool,' he said. 'The house is practically derelict. Belle's father died when she was sixteen and the death duties were fairly crippling. When we got married I think they were finding it a struggle to make ends meet, and soon after that the old girl closed up the house and spent most of her time at the flat the old man had kept in Bayswater.

Since then she's managed to keep the roof leak-free and little else.'

'And this is where she wants to spend her last days?'

Jake nodded. 'And Belle intends to go with her.'

'No kidding!' Shane stared at him. 'Are you going to let her?'

'I can't stop her.'

Jake spoke impatiently, but inside he wasn't so blasé. Dammit, Isobel was still his wife, and he didn't like to think of her and Emily stuck in some draughty old pile on the Yorkshire moors. Sure, the scenery was magnificent, and Lady Hannah still commanded some respect in the village. But it was fairly early in the year yet. Unless he missed his guess the place would be cold and damp. Living at Mattingley in its present state wouldn't be a pleasure; it would be an ordeal.

Shane shrugged. 'Well, you know your own business best, pal,' he remarked wryly. 'And I guess Marcie wouldn't appreciate you getting involved in Isobel's affairs.'

'Marcie has nothing to do with it,' snarled Jake, aware that he was being far too vehement in Isobel's defence. Dammit, Shane was right. Marcie wouldn't approve. But the truth was that was partly why he'd spent such a crappy weekend. This wasn't just about Marcie. It was about the unwelcome curl of heat he felt in the pit of his stomach every time he thought of Isobel.

And, after what she'd done, how sensible was that?

Isobel arrived home on Wednesday evening feeling as if the whole weight of the world was bearing down on her shoulders. Her mother was due to leave hospital in a couple of days and she expected Isobel to have already made preliminary arrangements to leave for Yorkshire at the end of the week.

Which was almost impossible.

Apart from anything else Isobel had yet to speak to Emily's head teacher. And, with the Easter holidays still a recent memory, she was hardly likely to look too kindly on Isobel's taking her daughter out of school again, for what could be an indefinite period.

Her own situation wasn't much better. Mr Latimer, at the agency, had warned her that he couldn't keep her job open indefinitely either. He was willing to give her a month's leave of absence, but after that he was making no promises. It would depend how efficient her temporary replacement was.

She had spoken to the Edwardses, but that had not been a reassuring call. Mrs Edwards was more than willing to welcome 'her ladyship' back to Mattingley, but she had warned Isobel that it had been a very damp spring and that they should bring their own bedding with them.

'I'll air the mattresses, Mrs McCabe,' she'd promised, 'but I wouldn't like to say what the linens are like after all this time.'

'That's all right, Mrs Edwards.' Isobel had intended to pack sheets and towels in any case. 'But if you could light a few fires and ask Mr Edwards to get the boiler working, I'd be grateful.'

The old housekeeper had promised to do her best but, as Jake had pointed out, the Edwardses were old, and there was only so much they could do.

What Mattingley needed was complete renovation and redecoration, but that was not likely to happen any time soon. Indeed, Isobel knew that when her mother died the old house would have to be sold. Any improvements would be the responsibility of the new buyers, whoever they might be.

She was making herself a sandwich in lieu of dinner when the phone rang.

She guessed it was probably her friend Sarah. Emily had gone home with the Danielses after school. Sarah's eldest daughter was just a year older than Emily, and not half so provocative. The two girls were good friends, however. Following in their parents' footsteps, Sarah always said.

'Hello?' she said, picking up the receiver.

She suddenly felt a twinge of apprehension in her stomach when Jake said, 'Hi. It's me.'

'Jake?' She managed to sound sufficiently doubtful, and he grunted.

'Yeah.' He paused. 'How are you? How's Lady Hannah?'

Isobel licked her dry lips. Like you care, she thought wearily. 'Um—she's okay,' she said, which was a ridiculous response in the circumstances. 'She—er—she's coming out of hospital on Friday.'

'Is she?' Jake sounded thoughtful. 'So—what then? Are you planning to travel up to Yorkshire at the weekend?'

'Maybe.' Isobel didn't want to think that far ahead. 'If I can get things organised.'

'What things?'

Isobel almost gasped. 'What's it to you?' she exclaimed, her stress levels rising by the minute. When he'd left the apartment nearly a week ago she'd been sure she wouldn't hear from him again. Except perhaps through his solicitor. He'd made it perfectly clear he didn't want to see her—or Emily—again.

There was silence for a minute, and she thought she'd finally gone too far. But then he said flatly, 'And how do you plan on getting up to Yorkshire? You don't have a car.'

'I can always hire one,' retorted Isobel, wincing at the thought of more expense. But she knew it was a source of annoyance to Jake that she'd sold her little runabout last year. It had been just one more luxury she and Emily had

had to forego to ensure that her mother got the operation she'd needed. 'Was that why you rang?'

Despite the effort it was taking, the coolness of her voice must have got through to him, because she heard his sudden irritated intake of breath. 'No,' he said evenly, spacing his words. 'It occurred to me that if you were planning on moving to Mattingley you might be grateful for the use of the Range Rover. It's bigger than a car, and you'll have plenty of room for luggage.'

'Oh.' Isobel was immediately contrite. It was kind of him to consider the practicalities of them leaving London, even if she couldn't prevent the thought that there'd be no chance of Emily embarrassing him again if they moved to Yorkshire. 'Well—I don't—'

'Think about it,' Jake advised drily. 'Unless you plan on hiring or buying a car for the duration of your stay. Mattingley is pretty remote. And somehow I can't see your mother using a bus.'

Isobel couldn't either. Always providing she was well enough to get around, she appended with a pang. And taxis were expensive. She hadn't even thought about how they were going to get to the hospital, for instance. There were ambulances, of course, but they were for emergencies, and Lady Hannah—

'Think about it,' said Jake again, when she didn't answer. 'If you decide to take me up on it give me a ring on this number. Do you have a pen and a piece of paper?'

He waited until she'd found the necessary implements and then dictated a number, which she realised at once must be his cellphone. She wondered if he'd given her that number to avoid a possible confrontation with his girlfriend. She didn't know if Marcie was living at his house, but she would obviously spend a lot of her time there.

'Thanks,' she said, when he was done, and there was a pregnant silence before he spoke again.

Then, with a brief 'Yeah' he rang off, and she was left holding the phone and feeling hopelessly confused.

Ironically, her mother had no reservations.

'Of course you must borrow the car,' she exclaimed, when Isobel broached the subject with her the next morning. 'What's one car more or less to Jake McCabe? If he needed it, he wouldn't have offered it. Don't be a fool, girl. It'll be far more comfortable than some hire car. And there'll be plenty of room for my things.'

Not to mention her and Emily's things, too, thought Isobel wryly, knowing her mother would never think of that. But then, Lady Hannah had always been rather impractical when it came to practical matters, and since her illness she'd come to depend more and more on her daughter.

Still, with the decision made for her Isobel was quite relieved to be able to ring Jake and tell him they'd be pleased to accept his offer. He agreed to get the car to her on Saturday morning, but he was in a meeting and their conversation had to be brief and not very satisfactory from Isobel's point of view. She had wanted to ask him about insurance and handling, but she supposed she could ask whoever delivered the car on Saturday morning. Besides, knowing Jake, she was sure he'd have covered every eventuality.

Emily was excited at the prospect of spending the coming summer at Mattingley. And it had diverted her from thoughts of her father. But she didn't remember the place at all, having only paid fleeting visits there when she was much younger. In consequence, Isobel was prepared for her to be disappointed—although the idea of being out of school for several weeks would probably prove some compensation.

The school had been remarkably understanding of

Isobel's position. Arrangements had been made to forward homework for Emily to do while she was away, with a reciprocal set-up for marking should her absence be prolonged. And, although Isobel didn't like to think of it, it was the only sensible arrangement in the circumstances. No one knew—or wanted to anticipate—how long they might be away.

Lady Hannah was released from the hospital on Friday afternoon, and although it would have been easier to bring the old lady to Eaton Crescent, the absence of a lift made that impractical. In consequence, Isobel did all her own packing on Friday morning and then she and Emily spent the night at Lady Hannah's service flat.

She didn't know what time Jake would send the car on Saturday morning so, leaving Emily with her grandmother, she left straight after giving the old lady her breakfast.

She'd only had time for a cup of coffee before leaving, and she told herself that was why she experienced such a feeling of dizziness when she walked along the crescent to number twenty-three and saw Jake leaning against the bonnet of the dark green Range Rover that was parked outside the apartment building. Dear God, she'd never expected him to deliver the car himself.

She was immediately conscious of the fact that she hadn't put on any make-up before leaving her mother's flat, and she was still wearing the lime-green shirt and navy trouser suit she'd worn to work the day before. She looked far too formal for the occasion—a situation that was enhanced by Jake's worn jeans and open-necked chambray shirt. His jeans were tight, and bleached in places she shouldn't have noticed. But when had she ever looked at him without remembering the lean, sensual body beneath his clothes?

'Hi,' he said, when she was near enough to speak to. 'I

was beginning to wonder if you'd made other arrangements.'

Isobel expelled the breath she'd scarcely been aware she was holding. 'I—no.' She halted as he pushed himself away from the bonnet. 'Mama came out of hospital yesterday afternoon, so we spent the night with her at the flat. It gave me the chance to do the rest of her packing. You don't realise how much there is to do until you start.'

Jake nodded. 'But you've done it now?'

'All but,' she said, gesturing towards the steps up to the house. 'Um—d'you want to come in?'

'Thanks.'

She was supremely aware of him following her up the steps and into the house, of his lithe athletic body mounting the stairs to the first floor in her wake. She managed to find her key without too much effort and pushed it into the lock, leaving the door for him to close as she hastened down the hall.

The hall itself was an obstacle course—plastic bags containing sheets and pillowcases and towels jostling half a dozen canvas bags that held most of her and Emily's wardrobe. There was a box containing Emily's computer, and several games for her to play, as well as CDs for her portable player and reading books. Isobel had tried to think of everything, but she was sure Emily would come up with something she'd forgotten.

'I guess you're planning on leaving right away,' said Jake, pausing in the doorway to the kitchen, and Isobel nodded.

'Pretty much.' She hesitated. 'The doctor seemed to think that if she insists on making this journey, the sooner it's accomplished the better.'

'Sounds reasonable.' Jake pushed his hands into the hip pockets of his jeans. 'It's just as well I came prepared.'

Isobel's jaw dropped. 'I—prepared for what?'

'To drive you up to Yorkshire,' replied Jake easily. 'I thought you might welcome a helping hand at the other end.'

Isobel gasped. 'You didn't say anything about accompanying us.'

'No.' He was honest. 'I guess I knew what kind of a response I'd get.'

'But you said I could borrow the car,' she persisted, aware that he didn't have the slightest notion of her reaction. 'I thought—'

'It's yours, as long as you want it,' he said flatly. 'I'm not planning on staying. Well, overnight, maybe, but I can always book into a hotel. Then I'll take the shuttle back to London from the airport at either Teesside or Leeds.'

Isobel shook her head. 'Why are you doing this?'

'Doing what?'

'Being so—so nice,' she muttered, gazing at him with wary eyes, and he pulled a wry face.

'Hey, I was always nice,' he said, apparently choosing to avoid any further embarrassment. 'Now, do I get a cup of coffee for my trouble? You do the necessary and I'll start loading this stuff into the Rover.'

CHAPTER SIX

IT WAS after six o'clock when they reached the village of West Woodcroft.

The small hamlet lay in a wooded valley to the west of the moor road between Whitby and Guisborough and, despite its isolation, it still attracted quite a number of visitors in the tourist season.

That was principally because it was one of the prettiest villages in this part of the country, with a tumbling stream bisecting its main street. In summer, the gardens of the cottages that faced one another across the stream were bright with flowers and at this time of the year there were still tulips and daffodils nodding in the breeze. The village also boasted a couple of pubs and a tearoom, which provided their guests with traditional country fare, and an old Norman church that dated from the twelfth century.

Mattingley lay on the outskirts of the village. Isobel had once told Jake that the estate had contracted a lot over the years, so that now it comprised little more than a dozen acres of arable land, with the gardens around the house left more or less untended. Mr Edwards did his best, she'd said, but the Edwardses were old and in no state to undertake any serious restoration of the property. Even if Lady Hannah could have afforded it, which clearly she couldn't.

It had been a fairly uneventful journey. Jake had expected Isobel's mother to kick up a fuss when she'd found he was accompanying them, but she'd proved unusually amenable. Perhaps she'd realised that there might be problems when they reached their destination, he reflected wryly. It was certainly true that he could accomplish more than a child and two women, one of whom was virtually helpless.

At least Lady Hannah had slept for most of the journey, which had been a mercy. Emily, sitting beside her in the back, had been forced to say little for fear of disturbing her grandmother, and Jake had had some time to organise his thoughts.

Not that he was any clearer as to why he had chosen to come all this way. Marcie, with whom he'd negotiated a fragile truce, had thought he was mad to jeopardise their relationship by associating with his wife. And even when he'd explained again that Isobel's mother was dying, she'd shown little sympathy for his situation. It was only when he'd added that this would give him ample time to tell Isobel that he wanted a divorce that she'd reluctantly given in.

Isobel, for her part, had maintained a polite silence for most of the trip, sitting beside him in the front seat of the Range Rover. He had thought she might take the opportunity to find out more about his future plans, but he should have known better. Either she was burying her head in the sand, or she really didn't care what he did. Whatever, she seemed perfectly willing to allow him to make all the running, and that irritated him a lot.

Yet he had to admit that when he looked at his wife irritation wasn't the first emotion that occurred to him. With her night-dark hair pulled back into a severe knot at her nape, his eyes were irresistibly drawn to the purity of her profile which, in the present situation, looked particularly vulnerable.

She had changed before they left, and she was now wearing a long-sleeved burgundy sweater over pleated taupe chinos that accentuated the slender elegance of her body. She looked pale, but determined, and he knew quite a ridiculous sense of responsibility for her. She wasn't his concern, he told himself. He was only here because it suited his purposes. But the fact remained that she disturbed his equilibrium, and the feelings of remorse she aroused in him wouldn't easily be displaced.

Even sitting in the motorway diner at lunchtime, eating sandwiches that had as much taste as cardboard, he'd felt that unwanted connection between them. And the fleeting trace of defeat in her expression tormented him still. He'd wanted to take her by the shoulders and shake some life into her, was tempted to grind his mouth against hers until she opened to him, if that was what it took to get some reaction from her.

Which was stupid, and he knew it.

Nevertheless, he was beginning to realise that accompanying her to Mattingley might not be the most sensible thing he'd done. Whatever happened, it was bound to bring back memories he'd much rather remained buried. His wisest course would be to do what was necessary and get out of there as soon as he possibly could.

He found the gates of Mattingley easily enough. Tall, iron gates, rusting now with age, they were set in a crumbling stone wall and stood wide, as if inviting trespass. But then, if what Jake had heard was anything to go by, there was nothing at Mattingley worth trespassing for.

Certainly the weed-choked grounds bore out what Isobel's mother had told him in one of her not-infrequent phone calls begging for money. Not that Lady Hannah would have called it begging. As far as she was concerned, so long as he was married to her daughter he had a duty towards Mattingley, just as Isobel did.

'Is this it? Are we here?' Emily had released her seat belt and was now leaning forward to wedge her face between the seats, her eyes dark with disappointment. 'What a dump!'

'It's not a dump,' said Isobel reprovingly, her eyes darting to Jake's, as if seeking his support. 'It just needs work, that's all.'

'It would take a JCB to clear this,' retorted Emily gloomily. 'I thought you said it was a beautiful place.'

'It was a beautiful place when your mother was young,' declared Lady Hannah, proving she was awake and had heard her granddaughter's complaints. 'And it can be again. With the right attitude.'

'And the odd million pounds,' murmured Jake, almost under his breath, but he realised at once that Isobel had heard him.

'We don't need your money,' she muttered scathingly, before turning to ask her mother how she was feeling, and Jake felt an increasingly familiar sense of inadequacy at her words. Which got under his skin. Dammit, he was doing her a favour here, not the other way about.

They bumped up the long drive that led between tall limes and oak trees that, like the rest of the vegetation, were badly in need of attention. An algae-covered pond looked dank and uninviting between the trees, and the stone terraces which had once been such a feature of the house were now almost unrecognisable beneath a film of green moss.

'Is the house like this?' asked Emily, and although Isobel hadn't said anything Jake guessed she'd been worrying about that, too. Her mother was a sick woman, and, however desperate she was to spend her last days at Mattingley, Isobel would not want to precipitate the event.

'Let's hope not,' he answered her, realising Isobel was having a hard time thinking of a reply. 'Still, you have to admit it is impressive, Em. And you're its only heir.'

'Unless you and Mummy have another baby,' she countered, proving she hadn't given up on her original claim, and Jake's mouth flattened.

He'd just realised how easily he'd called her 'Em', as Isobel did. The name had slipped naturally from his lips and he knew he had to guard against becoming too familiar with her. The trouble was, he liked her. He thought she had spirit. And why not? he thought bitterly. She was Piers Mallory's daughter and no one could have accused *him* of lacking in confidence.

'That's not likely, Emily,' put in her grandmother at that moment, reminding Jake that, however useful he might be to her financially, she still regarded him as an interloper. 'Now, hand me my bag, will you? We're almost there.'

To Jake's relief, the house itself looked fairly sound. Its mellow stone façade looked almost imposing in the last rays of the setting sun, its windows glinting like so many jewels in the evening light.

The house rose a couple of storeys above its ground-floor apartments, with two rows of long windows flanking the heavy oak door. Jake knew, because Isobel had told him, that the wings that jutted at either end of the main façade had been added in the nineteenth century, while the main building was some hundreds of years older. He also knew, from experience, that although many improvements had been made over the years, its draughty halls and high-ceilinged rooms were almost impossible to keep warm.

The door opened as the Range Rover crunched across the turnaround at the top of the drive and an elderly woman emerged. Mrs Edwards, Jake recognised wryly, wondering how Isobel could ever have thought the old housekeeper capable of looking after them. She was frail and stooped, and even Lady Hannah looked stronger than she did.

'You go ahead,' he said, when Isobel hesitated before opening her door. 'Get your mother settled. I'll unload the car.'

'I'll help you,' said Emily eagerly, and although he knew he should tell her to go with her mother and grandmother he couldn't find it in his heart to refuse her. He had the feeling that staying here was going to be no fun for the child, and he wondered how she was going to continue her education without any formal tuition.

Isobel paused only long enough to say 'Thanks' before slipping out and opening her mother's door. Then, after greeting the old housekeeper, the three of them disappeared into the house.

'What do you want me to do?' asked Emily, following Jake around to the back of the car, and he pulled a wry face.

'That depends how strong you are,' he remarked lazily, and she gave him an indignant stare.

'I'm very strong,' she insisted, and Jake smiled before starting to haul Isobel's bags and holdalls out of the vehicle.

In fact, she proved quite useful in helping him install everything in the vaulted reception hall, only pausing now and again to make some comment about their surroundings. He guessed she was doing her best to find something positive to say, and his admiration for her grew in spite of himself.

'Did you and Mummy ever live here?' she asked, stopping to regain her breath, and Jake decided to be honest with her.

'We stayed here a few times,' he said, feeling an unexpected twinge of pain at the memory. 'But our home was in London.'

'So why was I born at Mattingley?' persisted the girl curiously. 'Was that after you and Mummy split up?'

Jake sighed. 'Surely your mother has told you all about it,' he said, picking up a box of china and glassware that Lady Hannah had insisted had to come with them. 'Come on, you can carry those candlesticks.'

'Why has Granny brought candlesticks?'

Emily was briefly diverted, and Jake was grateful. 'Don't knock it,' he said. 'You may be glad of them if the power goes down.' He paused. 'Besides, they're very valuable. Solid silver, so your grandmother would have us believe.'

Emily was sharp. 'Don't you believe it?'

'I believe everything I'm told,' replied Jake drily. 'Now, don't trip. I know they're heavy.'

'Not that heavy,' said Emily scornfully. Then, just as he was beginning to breathe easily again, she returned to her earlier topic. 'Why wasn't I born in London? Mummy says it's not important, but I want to know.'

Jake dumped the heavy box of china on the floor of the hall and then straightened, flexing his aching spine. 'Because your mother was staying with your grandmother at the time,' he answered her truthfully. He grunted as his muscles protested at the unusual workout. 'Thank God there's not much more.'

'Granny says we shouldn't take the Lord's name in vain,' Emily reproved him primly, accompanying him outside again. She bit her lower lip. 'Is that why you don't like Granny? Because she's very stern and strait-laced?'

Jake couldn't stop the grin that tilted his lips. 'Don't let her hear you saying that,' he teased, but Emily wouldn't let him distract her.

'Is it?'

'Did I say I don't like your granny?'

'No, but I can tell. And its not just because you think she doesn't like you.'

'Isn't it?'

'No.' Emily sighed. 'All right, then, why doesn't she like you?' Her cheeks were suddenly tinted with becoming colour. 'I do.'

'Gee, thanks.' Jake felt an inappropriate surge of pleasure. Then, sobering, he said softly, 'I think you ought to ask your grandmother that. Not me.'

'But you know, don't you?' Emily persisted. 'Is it because of me?'

Jake closed his eyes for a moment against the anxious enquiry in hers. How was he supposed to answer that? 'I—no,' he said at last. 'It's nothing to do with you. It's me. Only me.'

'But why?'

'Hell, Em, can we talk about something else?' He slammed the door at the back of the Range Rover and stared at her with frustration in his eyes. 'Okay. I wasn't good enough for your mother, right? I'd been brought up in care and foster homes, and if I hadn't scraped into university by the skin of my teeth I'd never have met your mother.'

'So how *did* you meet her?'

'That's enough, Emily.'

Jake was saved from having to say anything more by the appearance of Isobel in the open doorway. Her cheeks were flushed, like her daughter's, and Jake guessed she'd heard the tail-end of their conversation. Well, so what? he thought impatiently. Why shouldn't Emily know the truth? Lady Hannah had had it her own way long enough.

'Is—er—is that everything?' Isobel asked, as he and Emily carried the last few bags into the hall, and Jake nodded.

'Apart from the kitchen sink,' he remarked drily. 'You must have left that behind by mistake.'

Emily giggled, and even Isobel's lips twitched with reluctant humour. 'Good,' she said, glancing about her as she closed the heavy door. 'Now all we have to do is unpack it all.'

'Where's your mother?'

'She's installed in the conservatory, having a cup of tea,' responded Isobel thoughtfully. 'It's the warmest place at the moment. Mr Edwards has started the Aga, but the upstairs rooms have barely got the chill off them.'

Jake frowned, reacquainting himself with his surround-

ings. The huge hall occupied the central portion of the
ground floor, with twin staircases that fanned around the
walls at either side before meeting on the galleried landing
above. The walls themselves bore the imprint of the many
pictures that had been removed and sold over the years,
and, looking up, he could see cobwebs hanging from the
eaves of the vaulted ceiling. Impressive it might be, but
cosy it was not, and the look he exchanged with Isobel
proved that she was thinking the same thing.

'So, where is the old girl going to sleep tonight?' he
asked irreverently, and earned a reproving glare from his
wife.

'In her own bedroom, of course,' she said shortly, bending to examine the assortment of bags and boxes. 'I've
brought her electric blanket and her own pillows, and Mrs
Edwards says she's aired the bed.'

'Good for Mrs Edwards,' remarked Jake, aware that
Emily was listening to every word. 'So, what do you want
me to do? Take some of this stuff upstairs?'

Isobel's blue eyes darted to his and away again. 'There's
no need,' she said quickly. 'I can manage.'

'I said I'd help you and I will,' retorted Jake, not quite
knowing why her words annoyed him, but they did. He
glanced at the child. 'Em, you go and keep your grandmother company while your mother and I start on the beds.'

'Oh, but—'

'Just do it,' said Jake, his tone brooking no argument,
and with a resigned shrug Emily obeyed.

Isobel permitted herself another look in his direction.
'Impressive,' she said drily. 'What have you bribed her
with this time?'

'This time?' Jake was offended.

'She says you've promised to send her some new game
you've invented,' declared Isobel, riffling though the bag

until she found the ones containing the bedding. 'Isn't that true?'

'Oh.' Jake relieved her of some of the heavier items and started after her up the stairs. 'Well, yeah.' He paused. 'She's damn good.'

'Does that surprise you?'

Isobel spoke scornfully, and he was stung once again by his need to defend himself. But this wasn't the time to start a discussion on why their relationship had broken down, so, shrugging, he said nothing until she'd led the way into the huge bedroom that dominated the first floor.

Then his thoughts were quickly overtaken by his unwilling admiration for the apartment. Worn and shabby it might be, but the sculpted walls and ceiling murals were still as imposing as when Isobel had first shown him round the house more than a dozen years ago. The four-poster bed was stripped, of course, which robbed the room of some of its grandeur, but the bed-hangings had been brushed and someone had taken the trouble to clean the windows and vacuum the rug.

But it was cold. Despite the fact that it had been a fairly warm day, the sunlight had barely penetrated Mattingley's thick walls, and the screened radiators creaking beneath an unexpected surge of heat had hardly raised the temperature.

'Do you think I should light the fire?' Isobel murmured, evidently forgetting who she was talking to, and Jake glanced doubtfully towards the tapestry-covered grate.

'Maybe not tonight,' he murmured. 'Do you know how long it is since the chimney was swept? There could be a bird's nest or heaven knows what else in the flue.'

'Oh.' Isobel put down the bags she was carrying. 'I never thought of that.'

'We can get a man in to check them all tomorrow,' offered Jake, depositing his own burden. 'I dare say there's someone in the village who could do it.'

'Or in Guisborough,' agreed Isobel, mentioning the nam
of the nearest small town.

'Right.' Jake gestured towards the bed. 'Shall we ge
started?'

Isobel's lips parted. 'You're not going to help me mak
the bed!'

'Why not?' Jake arched a mocking brow. 'It wouldn't b
the first time.'

Isobel's cheeks darkened with colour again. 'Even so—

'You're wasting time,' he said flatly. 'Whatever you
mother thinks of me, I'm sure she'd welcome the chanc
to have an early night.'

Isobel regarded him doubtfully. 'You're being nic
again. Why?'

'Maybe I feel sorry for you.' Jake used the words delib
erately, knowing that nothing short of anger would stop he
from looking at him in a way that was twisting his gu
'Now, do you want my help or not?'

Isobel's lips tightened. 'I suppose so.' She opened tw
of the bags and pulled out four pillows and an armful o
sheets and pillowcases. 'I can always expect the truth fror
you, can't I?'

'I wish I could say the same,' retorted Jake, not knowin
why he felt the need to be so brutal. But when the colou
in her face gave way to a strained pallor he relented. 'Forge
it, Belle. Let's just do what we came here for.'

There was a bittersweet satisfaction in assisting her i
making the bed, but it couldn't help but remind him o
other occasions when he'd helped her out, and of how the
had usually ended up. They might not have had muc
money when they had first married, but they had had eac
other, and even the most mundane of tasks had provide
an excuse for lovemaking.

Not that they'd needed any excuse, he recalled wryl
He hadn't been able to keep his hands off her, and tumblin

her onto a newly made bed had been the least of his sins.
He'd wanted her with a passion that had bordered on ob-
session, and pinning her beneath him, letting her feel what
her body was doing to him, sliding his hand beneath her
skirt—

He suddenly realised Isobel had been speaking to him
and he hadn't heard a word of what she was saying. He
had been miles away, his thoughts taking him into areas
that were better left undisturbed. But now he was brought
back to the present with an abruptness that left him reeling.

Coming round the bed, Isobel brushed him aside and
bent to tuck the sheet beneath a corner of the mattress. She
had obviously expected him to do it, and he cursed himself
for letting her distract him. But he couldn't deny that as
her slim fingers made neat work of the corner his eyes were
irresistibly drawn to the provocative curve of her butt beneath the taut fabric of her chinos. He was aware, too, that
his own pants had tightened for totally different reasons,
and the sudden ache between his legs was painfully familiar.

God, he thought, stunned by the realisation, he still
wanted her. Wanted to have sex with her, at least, he
amended impatiently, his face hardening in frustration so
that when she looked up at him all she saw was his irritation.

'Well, I waited for you do to it!' she exclaimed, obviously getting the wrong message. 'What's the matter? Is
manual labour too boring for the great computer expert?'

It was the wrong thing for her to say. He needed a scapegoat and she was it. 'What a sharp tongue you have,
Grandma,' he mocked coldly. 'Be careful, Belle. You're
turning into your mother before my eyes.'

Isobel caught her breath at his deliberate cruelty. But it
was as if he couldn't be with her without remembering

what they'd had; what they'd *lost*. And he was sickened by it.

'You've changed, Jake,' she said, finding her voice with an obvious effort. 'Is this what Miss Duncan has done to you? Or perhaps it was one of the other women you've slept with over the years. How many of them were there? Twenty? Thirty? No, I think that's too conservative an estimate. Certainly more than enough to compensate for one—supposedly—deliberate mistake on my part.'

Jake swore. 'Nothing could compensate for that, Isobel,' he snapped angrily. She had retreated round the bed as she spoke, but now he came after her, trapping her between the heavy canopy and the wall. 'And why are you interested in how many women I've slept with?' His lips curled. 'Be careful or I might think you're jealous.'

Isobel swallowed, tilting her face up to his with sudden passion. 'Perhaps I am,' she said, allowing him a glimpse of the unguarded pain that was darkening her eyes. 'There, that's something for you and Marcie to relish next time you're—screwing one another!'

Jake's stomach hollowed. He had expected her to deny it, to tell him she could think of nothing less likely to arouse her jealousy than the thought of him with some other woman, but her answer totally astounded him. Astounded him and left him hungry to do something about it.

'You're crazy,' he said, the hoarseness of his voice some indication of his emotional turmoil. But she stood her ground.

'Am I?' she asked steadily. 'Well, you would know.'

The hand Jake had splayed against the wall when he'd cornered her balled into a fist. He wanted to hurt someone, he thought—himself, probably—but when his eyes rested on her mouth it wasn't that kind of pain he was thinking of. Her breasts were rising and falling rapidly, proof that she wasn't as controlled as she'd like to appear, and his fingers itched to invade the neckline of her sweater and stroke the flesh beneath. Flesh which he knew from experience was smooth and silky. And soft, so soft...

'This is insane,' he said harshly, but he didn't move away. He couldn't. Besides, his erection made any kind of movement a torment, and what he really wanted was for her to touch him.

'What do you want me to do, Jake?' she whispered, and it was as if she'd read his mind. Did she know how he was feeling? Had she any notion of how dangerous this was? For him!

Yet his free hand lifted almost of its own accord and cupped her face, his thumb brushing roughly over her bottom lip. She quivered. He felt it in his bones. But she didn't draw away. She let him touch her, let him caress her, let his fingers perform their own particular brand of provocation on her skin.

And Jake's control snapped. With an exclamation that was more acceptance than denial he bent towards her. And kissed her. Hard.

He didn't know what he'd anticipated would happen then. Perhaps he'd expected her to balk at his behaviour, to be disgusted by his careless destruction of the fragile truce between them. Perhaps he'd thought that he would be so repelled by his actions that he'd be desperate to let her go.

What he'd never imagined was that her mouth would soften beneath his, that her lips would part and his tongue would be unable to resist the temptation. Like the snake he was, it slipped into her mouth, and he groaned at the sensual pleasure he felt when her tongue tangled with his.

Almost naturally, it seemed, the kiss lengthened and deepened, and it was only when he felt the lush roundness of her breasts against his chest that he realised she was now supporting his weight. Without him being aware of it his hands had dropped to the narrow bones of her hips, and from the way he was pressing himself against her she couldn't help but be aware of his arousal.

Yet it took the sound of Emily's voice, calling for her mother, to bring him to his senses. He could hear the child coming up the stairs, knew that at any minute she'd run along the landing and come into the room and see them. But he still found it hard to pull away. His body was programmed for a satisfaction it hadn't yet received. It took a definite effort to drag himself across the room to the windows, so that when Emily appeared in the doorway she saw nothing out of place.

'Mummy!' she exclaimed, and Isobel, who seemed to have recovered far more quickly than he had done, offered her daughter an enquiring smile.

'I'm here,' she said, infuriating Jake anew.

But then, she'd probably had more experience at recovering from awkward situations than he had, he thought, his mind returning to an old, familiar theme. God, how many times had he almost caught her and Piers together? he wondered. Whatever she said, he didn't buy into that 'once only' story. Piers had been a regular visitor at Mattingley. His parents had used to live in the district—probably still did, only he and Piers had no contact now. Isobel had come up here with her mother when Lady Hannah paid her annual visits. While he'd been working his butt off in London she'd been here, keeping her mother company. And who else?

Suppressing an oath, he turned and strode towards the door. He needed some air, needed to forget this crazy rush of blood to his groin. Maybe if he went for a walk it would clear his head. Right now, he needed to put some space between them.

'Daddy!'

Emily's disappointed cry found no sympathy with him.

'Don't call me that,' he snapped, not caring at that moment who he hurt, and she sucked in a breath.

'But where are you going?' she protested, ignoring the warning hand Isobel laid on her shoulder.

'Out,' he said shortly, his eyes savage as he met his wife's gaze. And, before either of them could say anything more, 'I don't want any company!'

CHAPTER SEVEN

ISOBEL awakened the next morning feeling as if she'd only just gone to bed. She'd slept, but only fitfully, and the sound of rain pattering against the windows only added to her mood of depression.

The conversation she'd had with Emily when she'd gone to kiss her goodnight hadn't helped. The little girl hadn't forgotten the question she'd asked Jake before Isobel had interrupted them, and she'd insisted on knowing how her mother and father had met.

'We met here, in the village,' Isobel had told her reluctantly, loath to remember how innocent she had been in those days. 'Your daddy was spending the weekend with— well, with some people he knew in the neighbourhood.' *The Mallorys*. 'Your grandmother and I were invited for dinner one evening and—and that's when we met.'

'And fell in love?' Emily had asked, still wide-eyed despite the lateness of the hour.

'Mmm,' Isobel had said non-committally. 'Whatever that means. Now, go to sleep, darling. We've got a lot to do tomorrow.'

After that she hadn't felt much like sleeping herself. The memories were far too painful, too acute to be ignored. If only Emily wasn't so interested in her history, so eager to make a connection between the present and the past.

But, despite everything, Isobel should have slept well. She'd certainly been exhausted when she went to bed. Aside from answering Emily's questions, installing her mother in the dubious luxury of her apartments hadn't been easy, particularly as Lady Hannah had found a dead cockroach in the bath, which she had insisted must mean that there was a nest of them hiding beneath the floorboards.

Isobel had checked as thoroughly as she could, but without proper tools, and with no real idea of what she was looking for, she'd had no success. It wasn't until Jake had got back and assured the old lady that he'd get a firm of exterminators onto it in the morning that she'd eventually settled down.

Which meant what? Isobel fretted now, as she crawled out of bed. Was Jake planning on staying longer than just overnight? And, more to the point, where had he slept last night?

Mrs Edwards had provided them with a hot meal, at least. Isobel and Emily had eaten theirs in the conservatory, after taking a tray up to Lady Hannah, but she had no idea when or even if Jake had had his. The table had been cleared by the time he'd returned, and Isobel had been occupied making up beds for herself and Emily. She had made up a third bed in a spare room, on the off-chance that Jake would want to stay here, but she'd left it to Mrs Edwards to offer him hospitality. After what had happened earlier she hadn't trusted herself to be alone with him.

Which was ridiculous, and she knew it. It wasn't as if there was any danger of him repeating his mistake. However violent his reaction had been to her deliberate provocation, he'd regretted it equally as violently. Just for a moment he had let her glimpse the sensual, passionate man she had married, before Emily's voice, and his own self-disgust, had driven him to put the width of the room between them.

Never mind the fact that she'd felt his erection hot against her stomach. He was a man, and men couldn't help their instinctive response to a woman's body. Any woman's body would have achieved the same result, and she could well imagine his revulsion at the knowledge that it was she of all people who had shamed him in that way.

She padded across to the window, drawing aside the heavy drapes and peering out. As she'd expected, she looked out on a grey world. Lowering clouds hid all but the most immediate objects from view, the rain-wet laurels and rhododendron bushes giving the place a gloomy air. Not the most optimistic day to begin their sojourn at Mattingley, she thought ruefully. But it was up to her to make the best of it, for her mother's sake if nothing else.

The water in the bathroom was cold, so Isobel contented herself with rinsing her face and hands and cleaning her teeth. Then, after dressing in a serviceable pair of khaki pants and a cream shirt, she went to check on her mother.

Lady Hannah was still asleep, which was a blessing. Isobel hoped she'd had a better night than she had. She glanced into Emily's room, too, before going downstairs, and discovered that her daughter's bed was empty.

It was only a little after seven o'clock, and for a moment Isobel was alarmed. But they were here, at Mattingley, she reassured herself. Surely Emily couldn't get into any mischief here? She was eager to explore her new home, that was all. Isobel could only hope she wouldn't be too disappointed.

As she went downstairs she heard the familiar creaks and groans that announced the fact that the boiler was working. Radiators older than Isobel herself were heating and expanding, and she crossed her fingers that there were no unwelcome leaks in the system, just waiting to confound her. Getting the old house into habitable order was going to take all her energies, without the added expense of plumbers' bills to add to her troubles.

She opened the kitchen door, expecting to find Mrs Edwards at the stove, and then stopped aghast at the sight of her husband sluicing his neck and arms at the sink. He was stripped to the waist, the shirt he'd worn the day before lying on the drainer beside him.

Isobel felt momentarily frozen to the spot. It was so long since she'd seen Jake even semi-nude. When he'd finished his ablutions and turned towards her to reach for the towel that someone—Mrs Edwards, probably—had left for him, she saw that his jeans were zipped but unbuttoned, exposing the arrowing of dark hair that disappeared into the waistband of his underpants.

Her mouth dried, and she wished she could turn around and go out and come in again. But it was too late. Jake had seen her. As he dried his beard-roughened jaw his green eyes caught and narrowed on Isobel's, and with a gesture of resignation he met her consternation with studied indifference.

Clearly he had had time to get his instincts under control, and there was no trace of either anger or frustration in his mocking gaze. 'Don't look like that,' he said carelessly, reaching for his shirt. 'You've seen me half-naked before. It can't be such a novelty for a woman like you.'

Isobel refused to let him provoke her. 'No novelty at all,' she assured him, coming into the room and closing the door behind her. 'Where's Mrs Edwards?'

'Where she usually is at this hour of the morning, I suppose,' replied Jake, buttoning his shirt with unconscious sensuality. 'Still in bed.'

'But—' Isobel glanced behind her. 'That is, I heard the radiators creaking. I assumed someone had started the boiler.'

'The boiler's been on all night,' said Jake, shoving his shirt into his pants and finally fastening his belt. 'But the radiators needed bleeding so that's what I've been doing.'

'I see.' Isobel shook her head. 'Thanks.'

'No problem.' Jake indicated the Aga. 'Do you know how to boil a kettle on this thing? I could sure use a coffee.'

'I do.' Isobel nodded. 'But there's an electric kettle around here somewhere. That would probably be quicker.'

'Cleaner, certainly,' agreed Jake drily, rolling down the sleeves of his shirt. 'Give me good old-fashioned gas and electricity any day. Solid fuel may be more traditional, but it's no substitute for convenience.'

Isobel frowned. 'Have you had to clean out the boiler?'

'Let's just say I've solved the immediate problem of getting the place warm,' Jake responded, starting to open cupboards and drawers. 'Where do you think Mrs Edwards keeps the coffee?'

Isobel was nonplussed. She had never expected Jake to take matters into his own hands as he had, and she wished she didn't have to feel so grateful to him. But there was no denying that Mattingley needed a man's hand. A much younger man's hand than old Mr Edwards was able to offer.

'So,' she said, finding the kettle tucked in a corner and filling it at the sink, 'have you seen Em?'

Jake pulled a wry face. 'I have,' he said evenly. 'And I assume you *didn't* send her downstairs at six o'clock to get a drink of water?'

Isobel gasped. 'A drink of water?' she echoed. 'But she could have got a drink of water from the bathroom upstairs.'

'Tell me about it,' said Jake drily.

'Well, where is she now?' She moistened her lips. 'She's not in her room.'

'I believe she's opening the curtains in the dining room and the parlour,' said Jake, making a sound of satisfaction when he found what he was looking for. 'I told her to get out of here while I had a wash.'

Isobel stared at him. 'You mean, she woke you up?'

'Did I say that?'

'No, but—' Isobel halted, and then started again. 'You

said she came downstairs at six o'clock. How do you know that? Did you hear her?'

Jake hesitated. 'I may have done.'

Isobel frowned. 'Look, I'm sorry,' she said. 'I know Em can be a bit—well, in your face. I never thought she'd go into your room.'

'What room?' Jake scowled. 'I slept down here.'

'You did?' Isobel caught her breath. 'But—I made you up a bed.'

'Really?' Jake gave her a funny look. 'I'm surprised. I half expected you to invite me into yours. Isn't that what you were hoping for when you jumped me in your mother's bedroom?'

Isobel didn't make the mistake of trying to slap his face. Instead, she gave him a look which she hoped told him what she thought of his childish suggestion, and crossed the room to take two cups and saucers from the cupboard. Then, taking the jar of instant coffee he pushed towards her, she spooned a generous measure of dry grains into each cup.

'Sugar?' she asked without expression, and he gave an exasperated sigh.

'Well, you asked for it,' he said, not answering her. 'Dammit, Belle, what did you expect?'

Isobel was grateful that the kettle boiled at that moment, and she could concentrate on adding hot water to the cups. How dared he suggest that she had 'jumped' him when what had happened had been all *his* doing?

Ah, but you didn't object, an insidious voice whispered inside her. She ignored it. It had been his call, she told herself. All she had done was—encourage him?

No!

'I asked if you wanted any sugar,' she persisted doggedly, and with a savage exclamation he took the hint.

'No,' he said, taking the cup from her with scowling

acquiescence. Then, as if needing to change the subject, he added, 'It's still bloody cold in here. Are you sure this is what you want to do? Stay here, I mean?'

'It's what my mother wants,' said Isobel, not finding it as easy to ignore his earlier comments as he obviously did. 'When are you leaving?'

Jake sucked in a breath. 'Well, that's cutting to the chase with a vengeance, isn't it? When do you want me to leave? Now?'

Isobel expelled a weary breath. 'It's obviously what you want,' she said flatly. 'I'm surprised you spent the night here. Particularly as you were so afraid to go to bed.'

Jake gritted his teeth. 'For God's sake, Belle, how was I supposed to know you'd make up a bed for me? We didn't exactly hit it off, did we?'

'And whose fault was that?'

Jake glared at her for a moment. Then his shoulders hunched. 'Mine, I guess,' he said, with unexpected honesty. 'Okay, what happened was as much my fault as yours. But how the hell was I supposed to react when you let me—?' He broke off abruptly. 'Put it down to frustration. I guess you can still rattle my cage when it suits you.'

Isobel gave him a narrow look. 'Is that supposed to be an apology?'

'Not an apology, no.'

'I thought not.'

'Ah—screw you, Isobel,' he muttered irritably. 'I've a good mind to leave you to stew in your own juice!'

'So why don't you?' she demanded, even though her heart quivered at the thought of him leaving, this time maybe for good.

But thankfully Jake wasn't quite that cold-blooded. 'Because you can't cope here on your own,' he snapped, swallowing a generous mouthful of his coffee. 'Not yet, anyway. That old lady upstairs needs more than you can possibly provide.'

By the end of the day, Jake was reasonably pleased with what he had achieved.

Mr Edwards had directed him to a firm of household repairers in the village who swept chimneys as a sideline and, with some financial encouragement, they had agreed to inspect every flue in the house.

Similarly, with his influence, the place had been checked by the local pest-control department, and no infestation of vermin or insects had been found. Their opinion was that the cockroach Lady Hannah had found had been a tourist, and that she was in no danger of being eaten alive in her bed.

For her part, Isobel had, with Mrs Edwards's assistance, spring-cleaned the morning room so that her mother had somewhere besides the conservatory to sit and issue her orders. The old lady herself seemed not at all surprised to find that Jake was still there, and he could only assume that she was prepared to suffer in silence if she thought he could be of some use.

His own energies had been expended in unpacking the rest of the bags and boxes that still stood in the hall. Fortunately, the night before he'd discovered a spare duvet among the bedding still to be dealt with, which was how he'd been able to sleep on the sofa in the morning room without freezing to death.

It had never occurred to him that Isobel might have cared how he spent the night. After that scene in her mother's bedroom he'd been furious with himself, and her, and he'd assumed she'd feel the same. He should have remembered: Isobel came from a different level of society, where childish tantrums could not be tolerated. However angry Isobel was, the demands of civility had to be maintained.

What worried him most was what would happen when he did return to London. There was still an enormous amount to do and, although the place was gradually airing out, most of the rooms were still in a dilapidated state of repair. It was crazy, he knew, but he couldn't bear the thought that Isobel was going to run herself ragged trying to do it all herself. Not when the expense incurred in hiring a firm of interior decorators would mean nothing to him.

He found an opportunity to speak to her just before supper, when she slipped outside to pick some daffodils that were growing wild in the kitchen garden.

Mrs Edwards was busy in the kitchen, preparing the chicken Mr Edwards had bought from a nearby farmer, and Emily was in the conservatory, rather ungraciously reading the local newspaper to her grandmother. Lady Hannah insisted the print was too small for her eyes, but although Emily had agreed to do it, she would much rather have been outside with her mother.

Isobel straightened when she saw her husband coming towards her, and Jake knew a momentary pang at the wary look that entered her eyes. Dammit, what did she think he was going to do to her? he wondered irritably. He'd been helping, hadn't he? Surely she recognised that much?

Deciding he couldn't jump straight in with his offer, Jake bent and picked a solitary bloom himself, handing it to her almost as a peace offering. Then, when she'd gathered it, along with the others, into her arms, he said, 'At least it's stopped raining at last.'

Isobel's mouth flattened. Then, 'Yes,' she said, glancing about her at the muddy garden. 'Mr Edwards says the sun will come out tomorrow.'

Jake couldn't prevent a wry smile. 'And he's the expert, is he?'

'No.' Isobel was defensive. She straightened her back. 'Have you come to tell me you're leaving?'

Once again, Jake felt that increasingly familiar twinge of resentment. 'Not tonight,' he said, answering her with the same edge to his voice. 'I wanted to talk to you, that's all. Without Emily or your mother in attendance. It's difficult to get you alone in the house.'

Isobel gave him a sceptical look and he knew she was remembering what had happened the evening before. The trouble was, he was remembering it, too, and it didn't seem half so reprehensible in retrospect. On the contrary, right now his fingers were itching to tuck the loose curl of dark hair that framed her jawline back behind her ear, and he was already anticipating how soft and silky it would feel against his skin.

His eyes dropped abruptly, only to be confronted by the equally tempting prospect of her cleavage, a dusky hollow exposed by the unbuttoned neckline of her shirt. Dear God, he thought, was this why he'd kept his distance all these years? Because as time had passed he'd suspected how susceptible he still might be to Isobel's unconscious sensuality?

But it was sex, he told himself fiercely. Only sex. And he could get that from Marcie. Indeed, it was probably because he hadn't had sex with Marcie in recent days that he was feeling this unwelcome attraction to his wife. He was horny, that was all. He'd get over it.

Isobel arched her brows now, and he realised she was waiting for him to get to the point. Besides which, there was a cool breeze blowing down from the moors and he saw the involuntary shiver she gave.

'I'm leaving in the morning,' he said abruptly, which wasn't what he'd intended to say at all, and he saw the barely perceptible tightening of her lips.

'You could have told me that inside,' she said, shifting the flowers from one arm to the other. 'I'm only surprised you've wasted a whole weekend on us.'

Jake knew she was only being defensive, but that didn't prevent the irritation he felt at her careless words. 'I thought you might have been grateful for my help.' he said, a little bitterly. 'I doubt if *you'd* have succeeded in getting the exterminators out on a Sunday.'

'Oh, you'd be surprised what Lady Hannah's name can do,' Isobel retorted stiffly. 'But I am grateful for what you've done. You—well, you've been a big help.'

'Gee, thanks.' Jake couldn't prevent the jeer. 'I'm overwhelmed by your appreciation.'

Isobel just looked at him. There was no doubt about what she thought of his sarcasm. She stepped forward, and her intentions were unmistakable, but when she would have brushed past him, Jake caught her arm.

'Wait!'

Isobel froze then. 'Take your hands off me,' she commanded, but a little demon inside Jake refused to be denied.

'Why should I?' he countered, looking down into her startled face. 'Isn't this exactly what you wanted?'

She gasped. 'You have no right to say that.'

'Don't I?' He gave in to the impulse to loop the dark strands of hair behind her ear. His fingers lingered against her nape. 'Wasn't it only last night that you told me you were jealous?'

She sucked in a breath. 'That was a mistake.'

'Damn right.' Jake felt suddenly savage. What the hell had she meant by saying that to him? She must have known what she was inviting. 'But it was my mistake, not yours.'

With amazing aplomb, she looked up at him now. 'Is that all you have to say?' She lifted her free hand and flicked his fingers away from her neck. 'I need to put these in water,' she added, indicating the daffodils. 'I think they'll look pretty in the middle of the table.'

Jake felt an unwelcome tightening in his gut, knew that if she looked down she'd see the treacherous evidence of he effect she had on him for herself. Yet she waited, oh, o coolly, for him to make the next move.

He swallowed hard, ground his teeth together, and tried o ignore her warmth, the lemony fragrance of the shampoo he used on her hair. But he couldn't help inhaling the eated womanly scent of her body and longed to taste her ipe mouth once again.

He knew she wasn't indifferent to him. Dammit, when e'd compelled her into his arms the night before, she'd een as eager as he to touch and taste. What bugged the ell out of him was why he would want to pursue that nadness. She'd been his wife, for God's sake, and she'd etrayed him. What possible novelty—and that was all it ould be: a novelty—what possible novelty could there be n seducing his own wife?

He didn't know. He didn't even want to guess at such a ick compulsion. All he knew was that his own control was vearing dangerously thin, and if he didn't let her go he'd ave something more to regret.

With an oath, he released her, but before she could dis-ppear into the house he spoke again. 'I want to arrange or a guy I know in Leeds to come and look at the house,' e said quickly. 'The main rooms have got to be made iveable.' And, before she could issue any denial, he added. Perhaps you should discuss it with your mother. Before ou reject my offer out of hand.'

CHAPTER EIGHT

BY THE middle of the following week, even Emily had to admit that Mattingley wasn't such a bad place after all.

As Isobel had known she would, her mother had accepted Jake's help without restraint, and she had had to stand back and allow her soon-to-be-ex-husband to put them even more deeply into his debt. Perhaps that was his plan, she thought broodingly, lying awake nights, worrying as much about his intentions towards her as the expense. Maybe he thought if she owed him so much financially she wouldn't object to any terms he offered her for a divorce. For, despite the fact that circumstances had made it difficult for him to talk about severing their tenuous relationship, she knew it was only a matter of time before the axe fell.

Nevertheless, during the day she was usually too busy to worry about her own affairs. Although she'd got her way in moving back to Mattingley, and might have been expected to be grateful for it, Lady Hannah was not a good patient. Even though there were workmen in the house, and some of the downstairs rooms were in a state of upheaval, she refused to stay in bed. She wanted to see what they were doing to her house, she insisted, and Isobel had lost count of the times she had to rescue the old lady from tripping over cables or being engulfed in the dust from falling plaster.

During those first few days they lived for the most part in the conservatory. With the windows cleaned, and new cushions on the wicker furniture, it was a pleasant refuge, and even the cool north wind that bent the plants in the shrubbery couldn't penetrate its walls.

106

It helped a lot that the sun had decided to take pity on them, and that the view from Lady Hannah's recliner was both relaxing and impressive. Beyond the tangled muddle of the garden, rolling moorland stretched as far as the eye could see, with just the occasional farmhouse or hamlet to punctuate the scene. There was a timelessness about the landscape, a sense that, however much conflict there might be in the world, these moors would never change.

The house itself was changing, however, though not in any fundamental way. All the same, Isobel had to admit that the dining room and the family parlour had been much improved already, and when the painting was finished and new wallpaper was hung, Mattingley would regain a little of its earlier style.

The gardens were another matter. As yet, Isobel hadn't even thought of tackling them. If they were here long enough she supposed she could hire a rotavator and try and clear some of the undergrowth. But right now she had enough to do, and the future was nebulous at best.

At least Emily seemed to have settled down in her new surroundings. It helped that Isobel had agreed that the decorators should redecorate her room, too. In consequence, Emily had spent hours poring over wallpaper catalogues, proffering her own ideas as to how the job should be done.

Jake, of course, had left on Monday morning, and Isobel had no idea if he intended to return. He'd given his orders—or his ultimatum, whichever way you cared to look at it—and departed for the airport in a taxi, knowing full well that someone else would be authorised to handle the final details.

Even so, Isobel had been amazed when a firm of interior decorators had turned up in the early afternoon. The strings money could pull, she'd thought cynically, even though she knew Jake had said that the owner of the company, Andrew Hardy, had been a friend of his since their college days.

Still, by Tuesday morning, a provisional work plan had been sketched out, and the painters themselves had arrived just before lunch. With half a dozen men working full-time it was amazing what could be achieved, and Lady Hannah had advised her daughter to leave them to it.

Of course, the old lady had instructed the men to be wary of the mouldings, and they'd been left in no doubt that this was no ordinary house they were dealing with. Isobel had once found her mother regaling the wallpaper-stripping crew with the history of Mattingley itself, describing the shooting parties her grandfather used to hold there before the first World War and boasting about the famous people who'd used to vie for an invitation.

Isobel was inclined to take her mother's stories with a pinch of salt, and she hoped the workmen did, too. There was no doubt that Mattingley had once been quite a show-place, but it had never had the reputation of Castle Howard.

By the end of the week the family parlour was finished and the dining room had had its walls stripped and the Waterford chandelier removed for cleaning. After the room had been decorated a French polisher was coming to wax the floor, and the upholstery on the Queen Anne dining chairs was being carefully cleaned and expertly repaired at Andrew Hardy's workshop in Leeds.

It seemed all too much for Isobel to cope with. Why was Jake going to such lengths on their behalf? Surely he must realise that when her mother died the house would have to be sold anyway? If he'd wanted to do something to make their lives more comfortable, hiring a firm of household cleaners would have been enough.

Always the grand gesture, she thought bitterly. But that wasn't really fair. Jake had never gone in for 'grand gestures'. That was her mother's domain, not his. And he was making her mother happy. Perhaps that was all he intended.

Her mother, meanwhile, seemed amazingly well. Moving

to Mattingley did seem to have given her a new lease of life. Or perhaps it was seeing the old house regaining a little of its elegance. There was no denying that it looked much different now from the neglected place it had been on their arrival.

Friday dawned bright and sunny and, deciding she needed to get some air, Isobel rallied Mr Edwards for an assault on the garden at the back of the house. This was the area Lady Hannah looked out on from her chair in the conservatory, and as her mother was still in bed, reading the morning newspaper, Isobel and Emily joined the old man.

A stone-flagged patio gave onto lawns and a shrubbery and, leaving Emily picking weeds out from between the stones with a spiked stick, Isobel and Mr Edwards started clearing the borders. Between clumps of rank grass and dandelions, delicate primulas struggled to raise their heads, and tulips and narcissus were exposed when the weeds were pulled away.

'You look busy.'

The unexpected sound of a man's voice startled Isobel, and for a moment she thought it was Jake. But his voice was much deeper, much less arrogant, without the mannered quality that spoke of a public school education.

She got to her feet, immediately aware of how untidy she must look, with her hair coming loose from its knot and her sweater and trousers smeared with mud. Thankfully, Mr Edwards had provided her with gardening gloves, so her hands were clean, but she couldn't be so sure about her face.

The man who had addressed her was standing on the patio, hands thrust into the pockets of brown corduroys, an Aran sweater not really flattering his bulky build. Not quite as tall as Jake, he was nevertheless not a small man, and his broad features were creased into a smile.

Isobel did not smile, however. 'What are you doing here, Piers?' she asked, aware that Emily was listening to every word.

'Hey...' He gave a petulant snort. 'Is that any way to greet an old friend? What do you think I'm doing here? I heard you were staying at Mattingley and I came to offer my help, if it's needed.'

'It isn't.' Isobel glanced significantly back at the flower bed. 'Thanks, but no thanks, as they say. I'm sure you can show yourself off the premises.'

Piers scowled, and Emily, who had no idea who he was, or how revolted her mother was to see him, gave him a rueful look. 'Shall I ask Granny if she'd like to speak to Mr—er—Piers?' she asked innocently, and Isobel wondered if she was trying to be helpful or just deliberately annoying.

'That won't be necessary, Em,' she said quickly, before Piers could respond. Then, pointedly, 'How are you getting on with the weeding? That seems a very small pile of grass.'

Emily pulled a face at her mother, but not before Piers had rewarded her with a smug smile. 'You must be Isobel's daughter,' he said, holding out his hand invitingly. 'It's very nice to meet you, Em—Emma, is it?'

'Emily,' answered the girl as they shook hands, and Isobel wanted to scream with frustration.

'Emily.' Piers savoured the name. 'How nice it is to meet you, Emily. I'm an old friend of your mother's. Piers Mallory. My family owns the property adjoining your grandmother's.'

Emily's eyes widened. 'Do you have an estate, too?' she asked, and Isobel guessed her mother was responsible for that.

'A small one,' he conceded modestly. 'We run a grouse moor.'

'What's a grouse moor?' asked Emily curiously, but Isobel had no intention of allowing Piers to use her daughter to prolong his visit.

'It's where they shoot birds,' she said, answering Emily's question herself. 'You wouldn't like it, Em. They kill the birds for sport.'

'Shame on you, Isobel.' Only the tightening lines around his mouth revealed that he was annoyed. He turned back to Emily. 'Your mother knows perfectly well that grouse-shooting is a necessary part of country life.'

'Is it like fox-hunting?' asked Emily at once, and Isobel had to hide a smile as Piers recognised he had made a tactical error. ''Cos I don't like fox-hunting,' went on Emily. 'It's cruel. I don't care if foxes are a nuisance. They have as much right to live as anything else.'

'Which shows that you've spent far too much time in the city,' declared Piers, rallying his defence. 'You ask your grandmother. She'll tell you I'm right. Besides—' he cast another glance at Isobel '—there's nothing like riding out with the hounds on a misty winter's morning. You do ride, I suppose, Emily? Your grandmother used to be quite a horsewoman when she was young.'

'Granny used to ride horses?' exclaimed Emily in surprise, but Isobel had heard enough.

'Never mind what your grandmother used to do, Emily,' she said. 'You're supposed to be working.' She looked at the man. 'Goodbye, Piers. As you can see, we don't have time for social chit-chat.'

Piers's expression darkened, and she thought for a moment he was going to ignore her dismissal. But then, as if deciding it wouldn't be wise to say anything more in front of Emily, he touched a mocking hand to his forelock and strolled casually away.

Once he was gone, however, Isobel found her taste for gardening had deserted her. She was trembling, as much with rage as frustration, and it infuriated her anew that Piers should think he could walk onto their property without so much as a by-your-leave. How dare he? she thought. *How dare he?* She would have liked to take one of the guns he used to shoot his damn game birds and blast him into kingdom come!

Tearing off her gloves, she dropped them into the wheelbarrow she had been using to collect the rotten undergrowth and, with a word of apology to Mr Edwards, started back towards the house.

Emily, seeing a chance to abandon her own task, threw down her spike and followed her. 'Where are you going?' she asked. 'Are you going to tell Granny that we've had a visitor?'

The face Isobel turned on her daughter was not pleasant. 'No,' she said sharply. 'No, I am not going to tell your grandmother that we've had a visitor. Piers Mallory is not welcome here.'

Emily looked puzzled. 'Why not?'

'Because he's not to be trusted,' declared Isobel after a moment, finding it difficult to find any words that described how she felt about the man. She took a deep breath and tried to calm herself. 'I'm ready for a break, that's all.'

She didn't know if Emily believed her, but she didn't much care. She'd never dreamt that Piers might attempt to rekindle their association. When her mother had begged to be allowed to return to Mattingley, Isobel hadn't even considered the fact that Piers still lived in the district. And, even if she had, after what had happened she'd have been sure he'd keep away.

Lady Hannah was just coming down the stairs as they came into the hall from the kitchen. They'd left their outdoor shoes in the boot room, but the old lady's eyes went straight to the smears of mud that adorned Isobel's shirt and trousers.

'What on earth have you been doing?' she exclaimed, heading as usual for the conservatory. 'You look like a mudlark, Isobel. I hope no one saw you.'

Emily's mouth opened and Isobel was sure she was going to tell her grandmother about Piers's visit. But then she looked at her mother and closed it again, lifting her shoulders in a gesture of submission.

'We've been helping Mr Edwards in the garden,' Isobel replied tersely, grateful for the reprieve. 'How are you? Can I get you anything?'

'Well, not until you've changed those dirty clothes,' declared her mother shortly. 'Emily, you can go and tell Mrs Edwards I'm ready for my morning coffee. Then you can come and join me. I want to hear how you're enjoying your stay at Mattingley.'

Emily exchanged a speaking look with her mother, and then said obediently, 'Yes, Granny,' and darted away without a backward glance.

When she'd gone, however, Lady Hannah fixed her daughter with an enquiring stare. 'Something's happened,' she said, with her usual shrewdness. She supported herself by holding onto the banister and waited impatiently for Isobel to answer her. 'You might as well tell me. I'll find out soon enough.'

'From Em, no doubt,' said Isobel bitterly, pushing the loose strands of hair back behind her ears. 'Oh, all right. Piers turned up about a quarter of an hour ago. He seems to think he can walk in here any time he likes and I'll just accept it.' She shook her head. 'He must be crazy!'

'Piers Mallory?'

'Do you know another Piers?'

'I may do.' Her mother thought for a moment. 'I believe our local MP used to be called Piers, too. Piers Otteringham.' She grimaced. 'But of course he died a couple of years ago.'

'Oh, Mama!'

'Well…' Lady Hannah gave her an indignant look. 'You asked me a question and I answered it.' She paused. 'What did he want?'

Isobel sighed. 'I've told you. He behaved as if nothing had happened. As if I'd be pleased to see him.'

'And you weren't?'

Isobel stared at the older woman. 'What do you think?'

'I think you could have done much worse than Piers Mallory,' retorted her mother staunchly. 'At least he has breeding.'

'Breeding? Is that what you call it?' Isobel was sickened by her mother's hypocrisy. 'He's a cheat and a liar and you know it.'

Lady Hannah shrugged, but Isobel could see that her words had found their mark. Nevertheless, the unaccustomed activity was beginning to tire the old lady. Her thin fingers were clinging doggedly to the stair post but she was obviously wilting by the minute.

'He had money,' she insisted as a final salvo. 'Mattingley needed money more than it needed another dependant.'

Isobel shook her head. 'You and I will never agree about that,' she said, taking her mother's arm. 'Come on. I'll help you into the conservatory.'

'I can manage.'

Lady Hannah tried to shake her off, but she was unsteady on her feet and was obliged to lean heavily on her daughter as they moved away from the stairs. It wasn't until she was settled comfortably in her chair in the conservatory that she was able to breathe easily again.

'Now I'll go and get changed,' said Isobel drily. 'Em won't be long.'

'I don't need babysitting,' returned her mother, plucking impatiently at her skirt. Then, almost reluctantly, she added,

'I know you think I didn't care about your happiness at all, but I did. If I'd known Jake was going to—'

She broke off then, but Isobel had to hear all of it. 'If you'd known Jake what?' she demanded, and the old lady sighed.

'If I'd known he was going to become so wealthy,' she said slowly, 'I—I might not have—behaved as I did.'

'Opposing our marriage, you mean?' Isobel frowned, but Emily's footsteps could be heard crossing the polished boards of the morning room and Lady Hannah gave a sigh.

'What else?' she asked, composing her face for the child's entrance. Then, with her usual acerbity, 'Go and tidy yourself, Isobel, do. Your appearance is an offence to your position.'

CHAPTER NINE

JAKE made good time up the M1. It was a while since he'd given the Porsche such a long outing, and the powerful engine simply ate up the miles between the service area at Watford Gap and the M18 turn-off.

He was balked a bit when he got onto the A1. But once he left motorways behind and got onto the country roads the Friday night traffic was lighter and much less aggressive. The rush hour was behind him now and it was too early for drunken joy-riders to become a menace.

A glance at his watch told him it was a little after eight o'clock, and he wondered if Isobel and her family had eaten yet. He guessed they probably had, and he was tempted to stop at the pub in West Woodcroft and buy himself a pub supper.

But a desire to get the journey over drove him on, and he turned between Mattingley's gateposts with a sense of relief. He hadn't realised until then how tired he was, and he wondered again why he had chosen to drive all this way at the end of what had been a bloody awful week.

Of course, Marcie wasn't around to voice her disapproval. He'd arrived back in London last Monday morning to find she had left for a photo-shoot in Jamaica and wouldn't be back for nine days. The message she'd left for him had been cool, to say the least, but in his current state of turmoil Jake had been only too glad for the respite.

Of course, she'd phoned him several times since then, no doubt regretting her impulsiveness, but Jake had his own reasons for feeling peeved. Marcie had sworn she wasn't going to do any more photographic modelling now that they were together, but apparently her lack of success in the TV business had persuaded her she'd be a fool to turn down such easy money.

Jake could see her point, but he chose not to voice it. In all honesty he was finding it difficult to drum up any strong feelings where Marcie's antics were concerned. He found her efforts to provoke him rather childish, and he was glad there were several thousand miles between them. Maybe by the time she came home he'd have recovered his sense of humour. Right now, he was out of sync with himself—and her as well.

It was this feeling of imminent chaos that had bugged him all week. Even work, his usual saviour in times of stress, wasn't helping, and those employees he'd come up against in the course of business had had to bear the brunt of his black mood. Even Shane had not been immune from Jake's acrimony, but unlike the rest of his staff he'd had the guts to ask what the hell was wrong with him.

'Nothing's wrong with me, pal.' Jake had rounded on him angrily. 'Nothing that a few intelligent decisions couldn't put right, anyway. It's not my fault I'm surrounded by morons. For God's sake, who do they think is running this place? Them or me?'

'I think you should chill out, *pal*,' retorted Shane flatly. 'What's wrong with you, McCabe? It's not my fault that your girlfriend has decided to flash her boobs for someone else instead of you.'

Jake glared at him. 'You know, Harper, if anyone else had said that—'

'I know. You'd have flattened them,' agreed Shane, not without a little bravado. 'But come on, Jake. That is what's wrong with you, isn't it? Dammit, I can't believe you're all cut up over that little—female!'

'I'm not.'

Jake was sullen and Shane's eyes widened. 'You're not?

So what *is* wrong with you? I can't believe you couldn't get laid if you wanted to.'

Jake sucked in his breath. 'Is that all you think Marcie and I have going for us?' he demanded, flinging himself into the chair behind his desk and folding his hands behind his head. 'What? I've asked her to marry me because she's good in bed?'

Shane had the grace to look contrite. 'Well, she's not exactly brain of Britain, is she?' he muttered unwillingly. 'But what do I know? I guess she's nothing like Isobel, and that's a plus.'

'You think?'

Jake gave him a challenging look and once again Shane was nonplussed. 'Well, isn't it?' he asked, staring at his friend in amazement. 'For pity's sake, Jake, don't tell me you're still hung up over your ex-wife!'

'My soon-to-be-ex-wife,' Jake corrected him automatically, and then dropped his hands onto the desk and sat forward again, hunching his shoulders. Then, 'No,' he growled irritably. 'I'm just—worried about her, that's all. Stuck up there in Mattingley with a kid and an old woman. You should have seen the place, Shane. Wuthering Heights without the modern conveniences!'

'You're kidding?'

'I'm not. If I hadn't been there, God knows how they'd have managed.'

Shane regarded him suspiciously. 'You're not seeing yourself as some kind of latter-day Heathcliff, I hope?'

'Please.' Jake swore and pushed himself up from the desk. 'Like I say, I'm worried about her, that's all.'

'Right.' Shane folded his arms across his midriff. 'So why didn't you do something about it?'

'I did.' Jake went to stand at the windows, looking down at the traffic so many floors below. As always, he felt the confines of the city pressing around him. More so now, after spending some time in the Yorkshire dales. 'I got a pal from Leeds who owns an interior decorating business to come and give the place the once-over. His men are redecorating a couple of the downstairs living rooms as we speak.'

'Sounds as if you've got it all in hand,' remarked Shane drily. 'I have to admit I wouldn't have expected Isobel to want your help.'

'She didn't,' said Jake grimly. 'If it hadn't been for the old lady she'd have told me what to do with my offer.'

'Ah.' Shane sounded as if he was beginning to understand. 'And that's what's bugging you?'

'No.' Jake swung round indignantly. But his friend's disbelieving face was his undoing. 'Okay,' he said harshly. 'Yeah, it bugs me. I don't owe that woman anything. Not any one thing, Shane. I just wish she was out of my hair.'

Shane pulled a wry face. 'Right.'

'Oh, stop saying "right" like some bloody counsellor,' snapped his employer savagely. 'I'm trying to do my best here. And she hasn't even had the decency to ring and tell me what's going on.'

'I don't suppose she knew she had to report to you,' murmured Shane mildly, and Jake scowled.

'That's not what I mean and you know it.'

'Okay.' Shane pretended to consider for a moment. 'Why don't you go up there and see for yourself? Marcie's away. She's not going to know where you are. Give yourself a break.'

Jake glowered at him from beneath lowered lids. 'Is that what you'd do?'

'Hey—' Shane held up his hands in mock defence. 'It's not my problem. I just think you have to decide why you still feel such responsibility for a woman you say cheated on you and, moreover, has had a child by another man.'

It was sound advice, but Jake had spent the rest of

Thursday and Friday morning arguing the pros and cons. He knew it would have been easy enough to find out what was going on. A simple call to Andrew Hardy of Hardy Interiors would have satisfied his curiosity about the redecoration. But it was Isobel and her mother and daughter he wanted to check on, and he had the feeling that he'd get no easy answers from his wife.

So here he was, back in Yorkshire, with no expectation that any of them would be really glad to see him. Lady Hannah might be pleased that he was checking on his investment, and Emily had her own reasons for wanting him here. But Isobel would probably see this as another attempt on his part to humiliate her. After what he'd said and done she had every reason to despise him.

If she only knew, he thought grimly, parking his car in front of the garages and turning to hoist his haversack from the floor in front of the passenger seat. His nerves were already taut at the thought of seeing her again, and he'd hardly given Marcie a thought since he'd got behind the wheel of the Porsche.

And how insane was that?

Deciding not to push his luck, he left his haversack in the car, thrusting open his door to get out. Just because Isobel had been willing to accommodate him last weekend that was no reason to assume she'd still feel the same. Their tenuous truce had been broken, and he didn't know how—or even if—he should try to mend it.

But he was here, for whatever reason, and he would play the cards as they were dealt to him. Shane was right. It was time he got Isobel out of his system. And if that wasn't exactly what his friend had said, it was the way he'd chosen to take it.

He had locked the car and was flexing his back muscles in the chilly evening air when the door of the house opened and Emily came rushing down the steps towards him. She

ad evidently heard the Porsche's engine and he wondered
f Isobel had heard it, too. If so, she was making no effort
o greet him. Perhaps she'd sent Emily out to test the wa-
ers, he mused bitterly, but the contempt that gripped him
t that particular thought was mostly for himself.

'Hi,' Emily exclaimed, omitting the word 'Daddy' for
nce, and Jake wondered if that was deliberate, too.
Vhatever, he should be grateful for it. She seemed to be
esisting the urge to hug him and jammed her hands on her
arrow hips. 'What are you doing here?'

You may well ask, brooded Jake, unwilling to examine
is motives at that moment. 'I—er—I want to see your
nother,' he said, raking back his hair with impatient fin-
ers. 'And your grandmother, of course. How is she?'

Emily looked thoughtful. 'She's okay. I think.' She
kipped along beside him as he started towards the house.
Is Mummy expecting you?'

Hardly, thought Jake, despising the sudden sense of an-
icipation he felt at the thought of seeing Isobel again. But,
No,' he answered evenly, glancing around and noticing for
ie first time that the Range Rover was absent. 'Where is
he? Where's the car?'

'Oh, she's out,' said Emily breezily, going ahead of him,
naware that her words had had such a violent effect on
er companion. 'Excuse the smell,' she added, as they en-
red the hall. 'It's the paint. Granny says it's a necessary
vil.'

'Good of her,' muttered Jake, struggling to control his
eaction to what the child had said. Isobel wasn't here? So
vhere the hell was she? Where on earth would she go with
sick mother and a young child to care for? Who did she
now in the district to be paying social calls at this hour
f the evening?

Piers Mallory!

Jake's stomach clenched.

It was crazy but even the thought of Piers Mallory caused an actual feeling of sickness in his gut. Despite the fact that he'd told himself many times that Piers had not been to blame for what had happened, he hadn't been able to forgive him. The other man would always be the bastard who had slept with his best friend's wife, who had cared so little for their relationship that he'd allowed a provocative woman to tear them apart.

Not for the first time Jake felt a savage twist of jealousy. Why had she done it? he wondered. What possible satisfaction had she gained from taking Piers Mallory into her bed? Despite the fact that when he and Isobel had been together they hadn't been able to keep their hands off one another, she'd spent her time at Mattingley seducing another man.

It was sick, and his skin crawled at the memory of how he'd felt when he'd found out. He'd turned up unexpectedly, summoned by Lady Hannah to drive her and Isobel back to London. They'd expected him on Saturday morning but he'd driven up on Friday night instead. And found Isobel in bed with Piers Mallory, too drunk—or too indifferent—to be ashamed of what she'd done.

Of course, he'd thrown Piers out of the house, threatening him with God knew what if he came near Isobel again, but the damage had been done. No matter how long or how often Isobel pleaded her innocence, he could not forget what had happened. In time, he had hoped he might find it in his heart to forgive her. He'd loved her so much and he'd wanted to put the past behind them. But they hadn't even been approaching that point when Isobel had told him she was pregnant.

Pregnant!

He'd wanted to vomit at the news. It had been weeks since he and Isobel had had any sexual relations, and in any case she'd been taking the Pill. The only explanation

he could find was that while she'd been staying at
Mattingley she'd been as careless with birth control as with
everything else. After three years of avoiding an unwanted
pregnancy, Jake had known it could only be her affair with
Mallory that had produced such a result.

There'd been nothing she could say to convince him otherwise. All the pleas and excuses she'd made at the time
he'd found her with Piers had seemed suddenly as empty
as her soul. However much he might have wanted to believe in her innocence, the idea of another man's child
growing inside her had been just too much to bear. He
hadn't even been able to stand to look at her, and so he'd
moved out of their flat.

It had been a terrible period. For weeks he'd hardly
known what day it was, drowning his sorrows in alcohol,
attempting to find solace in other women's beds.

It hadn't worked. Not least because he didn't like alcohol
that much. And the women he'd slept with hadn't satisfied
him the way Isobel had done.

His work had saved him.

When he and Isobel had got together McCabe Tectonics
had been in its infancy. He'd warned her that he had little
money, and that what spare cash he had would have to be
invested in the business, but she'd said she didn't care.
She'd even gone against her mother's wishes and married
him, knowing that it might be years before they could afford to have the family they both wanted. She'd worked,
too, and they'd pooled their resources, saving for a future
that had been cruelly snatched away.

Ironically, Isobel's pregnancy had come just weeks after
Jake's business had started to make real money. His first
venture into the computer games market had paid divi-
dends, and distributors had soon begun pressuring him to
expand his production. It was an area of programming he
hadn't considered exploiting until then, but in what seemed

an amazingly short period of time he'd started being considered among the first in his field.

If he and Isobel had still been together there would have been no reason why they shouldn't have had a child of their own, he reflected painfully. Maybe even this child. Emily. Who was now standing regarding him with anxious eyes.

She was probably wondering what she'd said to make him look so fierce, he mused, glad to see that Isobel had replaced the child's uniform with less formal clothes. In jeans and a royal blue sweatshirt, she looked like any other girl of almost eleven. Like his daughter might have looked, he thought unwillingly, tall and lanky, as he had been at that age...

He pulled himself up short. Now was not the time to be fantasising about her parentage. Just because he liked the kid, just because he felt sorry for her, that was no reason to become maudlin about the past. Besides, as far as he knew her mother might be rekindling her relationship with her father right at this minute. And why not? He and Isobel had separated over ten years ago.

But, God, he hoped she wasn't with Piers Mallory. The man whose name had burned an indelible scar across his soul. How would he feel if Piers was still unmarried? If he and Isobel got together? Not even the thought of Marcie would soften that blow.

'Mummy's gone to the supermarket,' Emily continued innocently, and Jake wondered if she'd sensed his anguish. 'She would have gone sooner, but Granny wanted her supper first and she said she couldn't eat while the workmen were here.'

Jake found his palms were sweating and he smoothed them over the seams of his pants. 'The supermarket?' he said, as if her words hadn't briefly robbed him of the will to function. 'Right.' He paused and took a deep breath. 'I didn't know there was a supermarket in the village.'

'There's not.' Emily smiled. 'She's gone to Pickering. The one there stays open late on Fridays and Saturdays.'

'Pickering?' Jake was stunned. 'Surely there are supermarkets nearer than Pickering?'

'Mummy likes the one in Pickering.' Emily was heading for the back of the house. 'D'you want some supper? Mrs Edwards has gone, but there's some cheese and tomato quiche left; Granny says she's allergic to cooked cheese.'

So what's new? thought Jake wryly, following Emily into the kitchen, reassured to find that some things didn't change. Lady Hannah had never been one to suffer in silence, and he guessed Isobel had her hands full trying to keep the old lady happy.

As Jake looked about the room, relieved to see that the place looked much more lived-in than it had done a week ago, Emily busied herself laying the pine table with cutlery and condiments. She set the remains of a delicious-smelling quiche in the middle of the table and placed a dish of salad beside a chipped china dinner plate.

'I don't know about this,' said Jake, feeling suddenly like an interloper, not at all sure how Isobel would react if she came back to find him here. He chewed on his lower lip. 'Perhaps I ought to eat at the pub. I can always come back when your mother—'

'There's no need, honestly.'

Emily was insistent, and Jake could see in her eyes the fear that he might not come back at all. It was flattering, but not the impression he wanted to give her, and his conscience plagued him with the knowledge that by coming here he was giving Emily false hopes.

'Look,' he began, but she wouldn't let him go on.

'I'm sure Mummy won't be long,' she said. 'Besides, don't you want to see what the workmen have been doing? Even Granny thinks they're making a good job.'

'Does she?' Jake grimaced. 'Well, that's good news any-way.' He paused. 'How about you? Are you happy here?'

Emily shrugged. 'It's okay,' she said, without a great deal of enthusiasm. 'There's not much to do, but Mummy says it will get better when the weather gets warmer.' Her eyes widened suddenly. 'Do you know there's a swimming pool and a tennis court in the garden?'

Jake did know, but he also knew that the swimming pool hadn't been filled for years. He feared the tennis court might be just as derelict. But he didn't tell Emily that.

'Impressive,' he said instead, giving her her moment of glory, and she beamed.

Then, realising he was still standing by the counter, she patted the table. 'Please,' she said. 'Sit down.'

Jake hesitated. 'I'm not sure your mother would approve of your feeding me in her absence,' he murmured. 'She may have other plans for this quiche.'

Emily grimaced. 'I don't think so.' She paused. 'I'm sure she'll be pleased to see you. We haven't had any real vis-itors since we came here.' She frowned. 'Well—apart from Mr Mallory, of course, and he doesn't count.'

Jake's stomach clenched. 'Mr Mallory?' he echoed harshly. 'You don't mean—Piers Mallory?'

Emily looked thoughtful. 'Yes, he did have a funny name,' she agreed. 'He said he was a friend of Mummy's but I don't think she—'

She broke off abruptly, rushing to the window and peer-ing out. As Jake fought the urge to demand that she finish her sentence, the child gave a delighted cry.

'Mummy's back,' she announced as Jake, too, heard the sound of the Range Rover's engine. 'Oh, she's going to get such a surprise when she sees you.'

Jake could believe it. Unfortunately, he wasn't as con-vinced as Emily that her mother's reaction would be a pos-itive one. Besides which, his own mood had soured con siderably at the knowledge that Piers Mallory had already attempted to push his bloody aristocratic nose into Isobel's affairs. He wished he had had more time to assimilate his own feelings before his wife returned.

'Shall we help her?' asked Emily, unaware of his turmoil, turning away from the window again. 'She'll probably have lots of bags.'

Jake shrugged. 'Why not?' he conceded flatly, following the little girl out into the yard at the back of the house. 'But your mother may not want my help.'

'Of course she will,' she said, giving him a puzzled look over her shoulder. Then, rushing towards Isobel, she chanted, 'Look who's here, Mummy. Daddy's come to spend the weekend with us.'

CHAPTER TEN

ISOBEL told herself she should have been prepared for this. She'd seen Jake's car parked in front of the house when she'd driven past on her way to the rear entrance of the building and she'd known what to expect. But when her husband followed Emily into the yard, and she saw his dark saturnine face illuminated by the shaft of light streaming through the door behind him, her knees went weak.

And, because of that, her response to Emily's cry revealed her frustration. 'Has he?' she said, opening the back of the Range Rover and beginning to unload the supermarket carriers onto the ground. 'I don't remember inviting him.'

'You didn't,' said Jake, and she was surprised to hear the anger in his voice. 'But apparently you don't have to wait for an invitation around here.'

Isobel straightened as he came across to pick up several of the bags and gave her a narrow-eyed look. 'I beg your pardon?'

'Forget it.' Jake started for the house. 'I'll dump these indoors, shall I?'

Isobel's lips tightened. 'I suppose so,' she said, not very graciously, aware that Emily was watching her with troubled eyes. Then, as Jake disappeared, she turned to her daughter and said quickly, 'How long has he been here?'

Emily pursed her lips. 'Not long,' she said sulkily, sensing a reproof. 'Aren't you pleased to see him?'

Isobel had no time to answer that before Jake emerged again, this time buttoning his jacket. 'I'll come back to

morrow,' he said. 'When you're in a better mood.' He
touched the child's shoulder. 'Bye, Em.'

'Wait!' Isobel couldn't let him go like that, though why
she cared was something she didn't want to examine right
now. 'I—have you had supper?' she asked, picking up the
remaining two carriers and closing the Rover door. 'We
can give you something to eat at least.'

'That's what I was going to do,' said Emily indignantly,
looking to Jake for support. 'I said he could have some of
the quiche we had left from our supper. But he said he
wasn't sure if you'd approve.'

He'd got that right, thought Isobel dourly, aware that
Jake was beginning to figure far too prominently in all their
lives. Why couldn't he have left them to make their own
way to Mattingley? Lent them the Range Rover, perhaps,
but butted out of the rest of their affairs?

Yet how would her mother have coped if the house had
remained as cold and inhospitable as it had been on their
arrival? Would she, Isobel, really have been able to mob-
ilise the tradesmen to do what Jake had persuaded them to
do? And on a Sunday, as well? She rather doubted it.

'I'm sure we can find something a bit more appetising
than cold quiche,' she said stiffly, and waited for Jake to
step aside before entering the house.

But at least he followed her inside—due, she suspected,
more to Emily's urging than to anything she had said. He
stood watching her reaction as she registered the efforts her
daughter had made, and then said quietly, 'This wasn't my
idea.'

'I believe you.' Isobel struggled to behave naturally, for
the child's sake if nothing else. 'But I've got some steak,
if you'd prefer it.' She forced a faint smile. 'Or are you
one of those real men who *do* eat quiche?'

Jake seemed to recognise her attempt at appeasement,
and acknowledged it with a slight inclination of his head.

'This is fine,' he said, as if unwilling to denigrate Emily's contribution. 'But are you sure you wouldn't prefer me to eat at the pub? As I'm staying there anyway—'

'You've booked a room?'

Isobel was aware that her response was far too revealing, but it was too late to withdraw it now and Jake arched an enquiring brow.

'Not yet,' he admitted. 'But I doubt if they're overrun with visitors at this time of year.'

'Well, no.' Isobel conceded the point. 'I'm sure they'll be glad of the business.'

'Why can't Daddy stay here?' protested Emily at once, evidently deciding her mother had forgiven her for inviting him in. 'His bed's still made up. You know it is.'

Isobel's face flamed and she struggled to concentrate on unpacking the bags. 'I know that, Emily,' she said tightly, feeling mortified by the child's submission and desperate to cover it. 'But—but your father might not be on his own. He may have brought his—well, his lady-friend with him. I'm sure Ms Duncan would find our hospitality less than— appealing.'

'If you mean Marcie, she's not here,' retorted Jake flatly, and despite herself she breathed a little more easily. His lips twisted. 'I think what your mother's trying to say, Em, is that *she* doesn't want me here.'

Isobel caught her breath. How dared he? she wondered indignantly. He must know she had every right to question his motives. She still didn't know what he was doing here. If he'd come to check on his investment then he could damn well turn around and go away again.

'I don't believe I said any such thing,' she declared now, anger giving her the courage to meet his mocking gaze. 'But I am curious as to why you'd choose to spend another weekend away from your—usual haunts.'

She had been going to say 'your girlfriend's bed', but

she had to think of Emily so she'd modified her words. Nevertheless, she was sure Jake knew what she was thinking, and she was childishly pleased when his mouth compressed into a thin line.

'Marcie's in Jamaica,' he replied evenly, and once again her stomach hollowed. So much for thinking he had some personal reason for coming here, she thought. She'd probably been right in her earlier assumption. He wanted to know how his money was being spent.

Realising they were both waiting for her response, she murmured, 'How nice,' in tones that indicated the opposite, and hated the wry expression that revealed he'd noticed.

'Where's Jamaica?' asked Emily, easing the moment, and when Isobel didn't speak Jake was obliged to answer her.

'It's in the West Indies,' he said, unbuttoning his jacket again and straddling a chair at the table. 'You know where the West Indies are, don't you?'

'She hasn't had your experience,' said Isobel tartly, unwilling to let him have it all his own way, and knew she'd scored a point by the look he gave her.

'I know where they are,' protested Emily, sensing another argument and trying to prevent it. 'The West Indies are in the Caribbean. Is that where Jamaica is, too?'

'Yeah.' Jake gave Isobel another wry look. 'Your mother knows that very well.'

Emily glanced at her mother, but when Isobel avoided her gaze she turned back to her father. 'Have you been there?'

'Yeah.' Isobel heard the reluctance in his voice now. 'So has your mother.'

'Have you, Mummy?'

Emily was gazing at her in surprise, and Isobel despised Jake for bringing that up. They'd spent their honeymoon in Jamaica: a trip that had cost them every penny they'd had but which had proved just as wonderful as Isobel had imagined.

'Once,' she admitted now in answer to her daughter's enquiry. 'On a shoestring. I'm sure your father's had other holidays there in much more luxurious surroundings than the Pine Key Apartments.'

'You remembered,' remarked Jake smugly, and Isobel's face flushed anew.

'You forget, I don't have the memories of dozens of other transatlantic trips to confuse me,' she retorted crisply. 'Since Emily was born we've had to conserve our resources.'

Now Jake's face darkened with colour, and not even Emily's presence could soften his response. 'I don't know why,' he said harshly. 'You certainly took me for enough when I got the separation.'

Isobel sucked back a sob. That was so untrue. Oh, sure, she'd let him buy her the apartment, and his contribution to their monthly expenses was generous by any measure. In recent years, however, Emily's schooling, and her mother's illness, had drained her financially—and emotionally—but Jake knew nothing of that.

Scrubbing a hand across her eyes, she turned to stow her purchases in the fridge, glad of the activity to avoid any further contact with her husband. But she heard the scrape of his chair across the floor, heard Emily's cry of protest, and knew what was going on. She could do nothing to change the situation.

'I'm leaving,' he said over Emily's tearful appeals to him to stay, and Isobel could only nod her assent. Let him go, she thought. She wished he'd go back to London. He brought nothing but pain and disillusionment to their lives. It was better that way.

She thought he took something out of his pocket and dropped it onto the table, but she couldn't be sure. Emily was crying in earnest now, and it was impossible to think of anything else at that moment. How on earth was she was going to console her daughter after he'd gone?

It wasn't until she heard the Porsche roar away into the night that she turned and saw his legacy to her. Lying in the middle of the pine table was a roll of banknotes. That was what he had taken out of his pocket; that was what he thought of her pitiful attempts to defend herself.

Emily had run outside after him, but Isobel knew there was no point in her doing the same. Not tonight, at any rate. Jake had gone, and the money—God knew how much there was—would have to remain in her possession until she could return it to him.

Jake was standing at the windows of his room at the Black Bull when the first faint streaks of morning appeared on the horizon.

Beyond the inn yard, West Woodcroft's high street was deserted as yet. It was too early for any shoppers to make the journey into either Guisborough or Whitby; too early even for the milk float that did the rounds as soon as it was light.

Not that Jake was much interested in the activities of the village. He wouldn't be standing here at all if it weren't for Emily, and he despised himself for his cowardice in giving in to the child's pleas. He didn't know what had possessed him to tell her that he wouldn't drive back to London the night before, and he decided that as soon as the landlord was up and he was able to pay his bill, he'd do just that. Staying here was only complicating an already difficult situation, and it wasn't fair on any of them to prolong it.

Isobel didn't want him here. She'd made that perfectly plain. She was probably making new friends. His nerves tensed. Or renewing her acquaintance with old ones. And, for all Emily had embarrassed her by stating that she hadn't stripped the bed he'd used the week before, he was sure that was more an oversight than a deliberate choice on her part.

So why was he hesitating in telling her that he wanted a divorce? It was what he wanted; what Marcie expected. And putting off the evil day wasn't making it any easier for him.

The trouble was, recent events had caused him to see Marcie in a different light. And, although he still wanted his freedom, he wasn't at all sure he wanted to marry a woman who had so little sympathy for an innocent child. And Emily *was* innocent. If nothing else, he had accepted that. It was going to be bloody hard to hurt her.

But it had to be done, he thought fiercely. Oh, Isobel had been clever, he'd give her that. She must have known how he'd feel, becoming personally acquainted with the girl, how difficult it would be to separate the real from the imagined. Emily actually believed he was her father. Whatever he did, however often he tried to deny it, she was never going to believe anything else.

Unless…

Unless he did as Shane had suggested and got actual DNA proof that they were not related. It was easy enough to do, for goodness' sake. A simple swab of saliva was all that was needed. Then she'd know once and for all that he and not her mother was telling the truth.

He shivered suddenly. He was standing at the window in just his silk boxers and, deciding it was time he took a shower and got the day moving, he started to turn away. But an unexpected sight arrested him. A dark green Range Rover was racing down the high street, and as he watched in some amazement it swung into the inn yard below.

Brakes squealed as whoever was driving brought the vehicle to an abrupt halt beside the pub wall. Jake winced.

He didn't need to see the registration plate to know whose vehicle it was. It was his. Or rather it was the vehicle he had loaned Isobel. What he didn't understand was what she was doing here.

Glancing round, he supposed he should get dressed. He doubted if her early-morning call was to the landlord, and he felt a certain unwillingness to be caught without his shirt again.

But he had barely had time to pull a tee shirt out of his bag before there was a tentative tap at his door and, deciding he had nothing to be ashamed of, he went to open it.

As he'd expected, Isobel stood on the threshold, and the colour in her cheeks deepened when she saw his bare chest and legs. 'Oh,' she said almost disappointedly. 'You're up.'

Jake inclined his head. 'Wasn't I supposed to be?' he asked. Then he saw what she was clutching. It was the bundle of notes he'd left on her kitchen table the night before. Had she been planning to shove them under his door? 'You hoped I wasn't?'

Isobel sighed, thrusting the notes towards him. 'It doesn't matter,' she said tautly. 'I believe these are yours.' She tried to put them into his hand but he resisted her. 'Please: take them.'

Jake took a deep breath. 'I left them for you.'

'Yes, I realise that.' Isobel's lips tightened. 'But, whatever you think of me, I've never been a kept woman and I don't intend to start now. All right, I know you're helping us at the moment—helping my mother, at least—but that has nothing to do with me. The allowance you make Emily is quite enough.'

Jake felt angry. 'That allowance is for you, not Emily,' he said harshly. 'And you know it.'

'Whatever.' Isobel waved the notes in his face. 'In any case, I don't want these.'

Jake ground his teeth together. 'Perhaps you'd better

come in and we'll talk about it,' he said, feeling the chill from the landing and realising that their conversation was probably clearly audible to anyone at the foot of the pub stairs. 'Unless you want the whole village to know our business.'

Isobel shook her head. 'Just take the money,' she said wearily, and Jake realised she was almost as tired as he was. Like him, she didn't look as if she'd slept, and she was still wearing the pale blue jersey and narrow-legged cord trousers she'd had on the night before. The fact that the colour of the jersey accentuated the incredible colour of her eyes was something he'd also noticed the previous evening. But they were shadowed now, and wary, and he couldn't deny the feelings of responsibility she inspired in him.

He reached out and, although he guessed she'd think he was going to take the bundle of notes, he grasped her wrist instead and jerked her towards him. Caught off balance, she stumbled, and Jake was obliged to put his arms around her to prevent them both from tumbling backwards onto the floor.

It was a mistake. God, what a mistake it was, he thought, staring down into those startled blue eyes and feeling the heat rushing to his groin. He pushed the door shut behind her, struggling to control his reaction, but just the feel of her against him made him ache with longing.

She was so soft, so feminine, so utterly desirable in that moment that he could think of little beyond the fact that his morning erection was suddenly stiff again and tightening his shorts. His whole body felt charged with emotion, and his hand curved automatically over her hip, bringing her into intimate contact with his maleness.

'Please—don't,' she said huskily, but Jake was barely listening to her. Instincts as old as time had him in their grip, and the urge to touch her mouth and feel the sensual

hrust of her tongue against his was almost overwhelming.
He already knew how she would taste, how good it would
eel to explore that moist cavity and bite the soft skin on
he inner curve of her lip. The memories were irresistible—
nd inescapable.

His free hand cupped the side of her neck, his thumb
ubbing roughly across her mouth. He tugged her lips apart,
exual anticipation darkening his eyes as he watched her
esistance. But common sense seemed to have deserted him
long with his control.

Her hair was loose about her shoulders and he pushed
is fingers into its ebony softness, feeling the dark strands
linging silkily to his hands. 'You want this,' he told her
hickly. 'Just as much as I do. That's why you came here.
Because you knew what would happen.'

'You're crazy...'

'Am I?' He drew her inexorably closer, moulding her
ody to his and feeling his own arousal getting dangerously
lose to erupting. 'Why not admit it? Or is that too close
o the bone?'

'I just brought the money back, that's all,' she insisted,
er hands coming up as if she would push him away. But
gainst her will, it seemed, her palms spread against the
rrowing of soft hair on his midriff, and the banknotes tum-
led unnoticed to the floor at her feet.

'Forget the money,' he breathed, when she uttered a cry
f protest, nuzzling her neck with his teeth. Then her rest-
ess fingers brushed the hard nubs of his nipples and hold-
ng out was definitely beyond his reach.

With the scent of her body filling his senses, he felt dizzy
vith his need of her. Wedging one leg between hers, he
earched for her mouth and was rewarded by the parted
eat of her lips. His tongue sank deeply into hot melting
weetness and he inhaled her essence deep into his lungs.
His manhood was throbbing, painful in its intensity, and he

gave an agonised sigh. He wanted her; no, forget that, he *needed* her, and, God help him, something had to give.

Beneath the pale blue jersey her heart was beating at a frantic pace, and when he inched the sweater up over her midriff he discovered her skin was as moist as his own. Perspiration dewed her breasts, their swollen peaks hard and vulnerable, and he discovered that in her haste she'd forgotten to wear a bra.

Isobel had always had small breasts, but motherhood had evidently added a womanly weight to them. As he gathered them into his palms Jake's senses jarred at the memory of her pregnancy, but the delight he felt in touching her again soon overrode any lingering restraint.

Besides, this was only sex, he told himself fiercely, as his mouth sought the sensitive column of her throat. Surely she could understand that, with her experience? He wanted to have sex with her, but that was all.

Yet as he overcame her resistance and peeled the jersey over her head, his hands softened, gentled. He caressed her breasts and her midriff and the slender curve of her waist with increasingly tender insistence. He rolled her nipple between his thumb and forefinger, enjoying the way she convulsed beneath his hands. And when he returned to her mouth her response was as hot and urgent as he'd wished.

Her tongue fenced with his now, tangled with his, and finally her lips caught his tongue and sucked it into her mouth. She had lost her inhibitions and she lured him on with mindless abandon.

Jake realised he couldn't take much more of this without losing all control. He wanted to be inside her. He wanted to bury himself in her heat and softness, wanted to feel her tightness closing around him and drawing him in. He wanted to come inside her, wanted to feel her all around him. He wanted to drive her to the very limit of her endurance and feel her orgasm joining his...

With his mouth still covering hers, he backed her towards his bed, feeling a sense of satisfaction when she subsided onto it. But she was still sitting up when he came down beside her, and he released her mouth to take one rosy nipple between his teeth.

The sound she made when he sucked upon it was a potent stimulant, and he eased her back against the tumbled sheets and straddled her body with his. Her eyes were somnolent now, and he recognised in them the same sexual intoxication he was sure she must see in his. Her actions were no longer governed by her mind but by her senses, and he took great pleasure in unbuttoning her trousers and slipping his hand beneath the lacy briefs she wore underneath.

She was wet. The briefs were damp around the crotch, and when he eased his fingers between the soft folds of flesh, he found a burning need to match his own. She jerked beneath him, her legs splaying to give him greater access, and her moan of protest when he withdrew his hand was transparent in its intent.

'Don't worry. I'm not going anywhere,' he told her thickly, moving aside to pull the tight-fitting trousers down her slim legs. The briefs went with them and he quickly shed his boxers. Then there was nothing between them but the urgency of their own needs.

Jake sucked in a breath when Isobel arched towards him. Her fingers reached for him, caressed him, blew his senses away with her eagerness to show him she remembered his needs as well as her own. 'Take it easy,' he said huskily, but she wasn't listening to him. Lifting her head, she pressed her mouth to his, and the agony of suppressing his need became too much for him to prolong the suspense.

'No more,' he groaned, drawing back and spreading her legs for his delectation. Then, in one swift, satisfying move, he thrust into her, expanding her and filling her as he'd wanted to do since he first went to her apartment.

She was tight, so tight. It was almost like making love to a virgin. If he'd had any doubts about her celibacy in the years since their separation they were instantly assuaged by the sudden gasp she gave when he pushed into her.

'Did I hurt you?' he demanded, his own desires briefly thwarted by his concern for her, but Isobel just gulped again and shook her head.

'No, *no*!' she exclaimed, convincing him she meant it and with a groan of satisfaction he began to move.

The pleasure was intense. But much too short-lived. He'd wanted to make it last, to find the dark peace of mutual passion in her inviting body, but his own flesh betrayed him. Even moving at all had him gasping for breath, and he could feel his control slipping away.

He knew he should draw back, that common sense demanded he protect her from herself, but he also knew he wasn't going to be able to do it. Heaven can't be any better than this, he thought, as the devil inside him triumphed. He wanted her; he wanted to spill his seed inside her. And if that was a sin, so be it. He'd take his punishment like a man.

But he'd have this to remember first.

And just as he felt his own climax approaching he felt her muscles tightening around him. She was bucking beneath him, her nails digging into his shoulders, her legs wrapped tightly around his waist. But it was the little cries she was making that were causing Jake to lose his reason. Dear God, he thought incredulously, she was going to be with him every step of the way.

The experience was everything he'd hoped for. Shuddering in the aftermath of his release, Jake lifted his face from her breasts and knew he'd lost. Yet at that moment with his soul cleansed of even the most minute regrets, he couldn't be sorry. She was his, he thought fiercely. His lover; his woman. His lips twisted. The only woman he had ever loved.

Isobel's eyes were closed and he wished she'd open them. He wanted to tell her how he felt, wanted to share with her the revelation he had just had. But she seemed to have fallen asleep and he couldn't disturb her. The shadows beneath her eyes were a potent reminder of the night they had both spent.

And what about Emily? his conscience probed, as he propped himself up on one elbow and looked down at her. Could he possibly be the child's father? Did he really want to know? Wouldn't it be simpler to accept that she was Isobel's daughter? That because she was part of Isobel he'd love her, whoever her father was?

CHAPTER ELEVEN

ISOBEL slipped out of the inn while Jake was in the shower. Somehow she'd managed to convince him that she was asleep, but as soon as she felt him slide off the bed and go into the bathroom she made a scramble for her clothes.

It hadn't been difficult to feign exhaustion. Indeed, she would have liked nothing so much as to curl into a ball and sleep the day away. But that was just a desire to put off thinking about the future. Although she'd just experienced the most devastating sex she'd had in her life, she knew as far as Jake was concerned she had simply acted as a substitute for Marcie Duncan.

Which hurt. It hurt a lot.

She let herself out of Jake's room and scurried down the stairs to the bar below, where she encountered Tom Cooper, the innkeeper. She dreaded to think what he must think of her, but she couldn't worry about that now. He'd been waiting for a delivery from the brewery when she'd arrived, which was how she'd been able to slip into the pub without being seen. But now he offered her a polite 'Good morning', as if he wasn't already speculating about what she and his unexpected guest had been doing.

As if there was any doubt, Isobel thought, sliding behind the wheel of the Range Rover and twisting the rearview mirror towards her. She viewed her reflection with disgust. There were stubble burns on her cheeks and her mouth was red and swollen. She might as well have hung out a sign that said 'This woman has just been well and truly—'

She balked at the ugly word that most fitted the situation and, swinging out of the inn yard, almost collided with the brewery wagon that was approaching down the narrow street. The driver sounded his horn and she only just prevented herself from showing him a finger. For heaven's sake, she chided herself, what was wrong with her? Laceys—and she would soon be a Lacey again, if Jake had his way—didn't do that sort of thing.

She glanced at her watch to distract herself. It seemed incredible but it wasn't even eight o'clock. She already felt as if she'd done a day's work and the day hadn't even started yet. She hoped Emily and her mother were still asleep. She had no desire to have to explain herself to them.

Fortunately, she'd told no one about the money. Emily had been too upset to notice the night before, and Isobel had shoved it into her pocket before the child began asking questions she couldn't answer. Well, Jake had got it back now, she thought; in spades. She just hoped he thought he was worth it.

To her relief, only Mrs Edwards was in the kitchen when she let herself into the house. The old housekeeper was in the process of putting a tray of bread rolls into the Aga's oven and her eyes widened in surprise when Isobel came in.

'You're an early bird,' she said, closing the oven door and straightening cheerfully. 'If you've been down to the stores, I could have told you they don't open before nine o'clock on a Saturday.'

Saved by the stores, thought Isobel ruefully, managing a smile. 'I should have remembered,' she said, hoping Mrs Edwards wouldn't ask her what she'd gone there for. 'Um—is Emily up yet?'

'I haven't seen her,' replied the housekeeper, and Isobel was briefly diverted by the memory of Emily's tearful face the night before. She hoped her daughter had got over her upset. Perhaps she'd thought that getting Jake to agree to stay overnight would make a difference. But after this

morning's—what? Scene? Seduction? *Sex?*—she doubted
her husband would waste any time before heading back to
town.

Deciding she needed a shower before she had to face her
mother's questions, Isobel headed upstairs to her room. At
least Mrs Edwards hadn't noticed anything amiss. Hoping
she could immerse herself in hot water and give herself an
excuse for her flushed face, she quickly stripped off her
clothes.

'Mummy?'

Emily's voice behind her had Isobel reaching automatically for something to cover herself, and, clutching the bedspread to her chest, she turned to face the child who was
still in her Winnie the Pooh pyjamas. 'Yes?'

'Do you think Daddy will come and see us again before
he goes back to London?' asked Emily, a tremor in her
voice, and Isobel heaved a long sigh before replying.

'I—don't know,' she said honestly, even though she was
fairly sure that the answer would be no. She put a nervous
hand to her cheek. 'Er—did he say what he was going to
do?'

'No.' Emily sniffed. Then another thought appeared to
occur to her. 'But he wouldn't have stayed if he didn't want
to see us again, would he?'

Isobel shook her head. Who knew what Jake planned to
do? She hesitated before saying weakly, 'Perhaps not,' and
was rewarded by the dawning relief in her daughter's face.

'That's what I think,' said Emily firmly. And, as if just
noticing her mother's face, 'Is your face sore?'

'I—it's just some moisturiser I used last night,' lied
Isobel unhappily. 'Why don't you go and get dressed while
I take my shower?'

Emily frowned. 'All right,' she said slowly, but her
mother doubted she'd heard the last about any of this. 'I
you're sure you're okay?'

'I'm fine,' Isobel told her tightly. 'Close the door on your way out.'

By the time Isobel had had her shower and dressed again, this time in a sage-green skirt and vest over a lemon shirt, her mother was awake and querulous.

'Why didn't you tell me Jake was here last night?' she demanded when Isobel carried in her breakfast tray, revealing that once again Emily hadn't been able to keep her mouth shut. 'I would have liked to see him.'

Isobel set the tray on the end of the bed and helped the old lady up against her pillows. Then, settling the tray across her lap, she said, 'He didn't stay long.'

'Is that supposed to be an excuse?' exclaimed Lady Hannah, flicking a disparaging finger at her egg. 'And this is too soft. How many times do I have to tell you? I prefer the yolk to be slightly firmer than soft.'

Isobel's lips compressed. 'I'm sorry. I'll make sure it doesn't happen again.'

'Do.' Her mother regarded her suspiciously. 'Are you humouring me?'

Isobel grimaced. 'A little, perhaps.'

'Mmm.' Lady Hannah picked up her orange juice and took a sip. 'So what did he want?'

Isobel was tempted to say Who? But she knew that would only infuriate her mother still more. So she tried to be as honest as she could. 'I think he came to—to assure himself that we're managing okay,' she replied evenly. 'Is there anything else I can do for you?'

'Yes.' Her mother gave her a studied look. 'You can tell me why you've got all that make-up on your face. Is it to impress your husband?'

As if!

Isobel swallowed. She should have known her mother would notice that she'd lathered a load of foundation over her skin. Feigning ignorance, she glanced at her reflection in the mirror. 'Oh, yes,' she said. 'I have overdone it a little, haven't I?'

'Just a little,' agreed Lady Hannah drily. Then, returning to her original theme, she added, 'Don't tell me it was your idea that your husband stayed at the Black Bull last night?' She snorted. 'I can just imagine what Tom Cooper must think about that.'

But not what he'd think about her daughter paying Jake an early-morning visit, thought Isobel with some relief. Well, not unless that particular piece of gossip found its way to Mattingley. She dreaded to think what her mother would think of that insanity.

'I—it was his idea,' she said now, stretching the truth. Then, because she had to ask, 'Why did you want to see him?'

'That's my business,' retorted the old lady tartly. 'If he comes back this morning, send him up here.'

It was the last thing Isobel wanted to do. But the command had a deeper significance. 'Aren't you getting up?' she asked, frowning, and Lady Hannah gave an impatient wave of her hand.

'Not this morning,' she said, pouring herself a cup of coffee with a hand that Isobel saw with some dismay wasn't quite steady. 'I'll get up later.'

'But you're all right, aren't you?' Isobel persisted, unwilling to leave it at that, and the old lady sighed.

'As all right as anyone in my position can be,' she replied crisply. 'Stop fussing, Isobel. I'm not dying yet.'

Despite her conviction that they had seen the last of Jake for the time being, Isobel spent the morning in a state of nervous tension. It didn't help that Emily skipped to the window every time she thought she heard a car, or that the decorators had chosen that morning to sand the dining room floor. The buzz of the sander and the sound of the men's heels clumping across the floor was a constant clamour, and by mid-morning her head was throbbing.

And just when she'd thought things couldn't get any worse Piers Mallory arrived. He stepped through the open door into the hall, his arms filled with an enormous bouquet of flowers.

Isobel had been upstairs, checking on her mother, and she was halfway down again when he appeared. Her blood boiled at the arrogant way he entered the house. All right, the doors were open to allow the workmen easy access, but he had no right to take advantage of it. Indeed, after what she'd told him the day before, she was amazed that he'd dared to come back.

He hadn't seen her yet, and she resented the way he glanced about him, as if assessing what had already been done and what was needed. Didn't he understand plain English? She didn't want him here.

She was in no mood to be tolerant. 'What the hell do you think you're doing?' she demanded, running down the final few stairs. 'Get out of here. Right now.'

Piers made no move to obey her. 'Good morning, Isobel,' he said, just as if she hadn't spoken. 'How's your mother today?'

'Don't pretend you care about my mother,' she exclaimed harshly. Then, half afraid the old lady might hear them, she grabbed his arm and attempted to hustle him towards the door. 'I want you to go.'

It was a useless exercise. Piers just dug in his heels and remained where he was. And, to her horror, he was taking advantage of her efforts to look down her cleavage.

'I'll call for help,' she threatened, stepping back from him, wondering if the decorators would come to her aid. But Piers only laughed.

'Oh, Issie,' he said, making her cringe with his name for her, 'what am I doing? Attacking you with flowers?'

Isobel clenched her fists. 'You have no right to come here. You're not welcome.'

Piers's lips tightened. 'So you say.' He paused. 'In any case, I didn't come to see you. I came to see Lady Hannah. Where is she?'

'That's none of your business,' Isobel retorted, steeling herself against the urge to glance up the stairs towards her mother's room. 'Will you go?'

'Not until I've given these to your mother,' declared Piers inflexibly, indicating the flowers. 'Surely you wouldn't deprive her of such a generous gift?'

Isobel's jaw compressed. 'I'll give them to her,' she said, snatching the bouquet out of his arms. 'Now, will you get out of here?'

Piers still made no move to go. 'You're not very polite, Issie,' he said, his eyes making an insolent appraisal of her body. 'And I think you've put on some weight, if I'm not mistaken. You'll have to watch that. You're not getting any younger, you know.'

Isobel wanted to scream. What did she have to do to get rid of him? she wondered. The man was completely impervious to her demands. Had he no shame?

And then she heard Emily's feet coming down the stairs. The little girl was running and Isobel had no chance of stopping her before she burst out excitedly, 'Was that Daddy's car?' Then she saw Piers and her expression changed. 'Oh, it's only you.'

'Only me,' agreed Piers pleasantly, and Isobel was amazed that he could sound so amiable in the face of such obvious disappointment. 'Hello, Emily.'

''lo.' Emily gave him a brief smile and then sidled up to her mother. 'I thought it was Daddy.'

Piers's brows rose. 'Your daddy's here?' he asked in surprise. 'I thought I must have been mistaken before.' His tongue circled his thick lips. 'Do I scent a reconciliation?'

'You don't scent anything,' retorted Isobel coldly. 'But Jake will be here at any moment. I think you should leave.'

'Oh, I think not.' Piers didn't seem at all concerned that the other man might turn up at any time. 'If McCabe was in the district, I'm sure I would have heard about it.'

Emily frowned. 'Did you come here to see Daddy?' she asked innocently, and Isobel felt the incipient threat of hysteria rising in her throat.

'No, to see your granny,' declared Piers, seeing the opportunity and taking it. 'Is she up?'

'Piers—'

But Emily's voice overrode Isobel's final appeal. 'No. She's spending the morning in bed,' she replied gravely. 'Would you like to go up and see her?'

'Emily!'

'That sounds like a good idea,' Piers affirmed smugly. He gestured her ahead of him. 'Will you lead the way?'

Emily looked a little uncertain now. 'Are you coming, Mummy?' she asked hopefully, and then seemed to notice the flowers in Isobel's arms. 'Oh, aren't they lovely?' She looked at Piers again with more enthusiasm. 'Did you bring them?'

'I did.' Piers smiled. 'Shall we leave your mother to put them in water?'

'Mummy?'

Emily was anxious, Isobel knew, but she found herself unable to speak. Shaking her head, she turned away, and not without some misgivings, she was sure, her daughter led their visitor upstairs.

There was a strange car parked alongside the vans belonging to the tradesmen when Jake arrived at Mattingley later that morning, but he wasn't concerned. It was probably the doctor, he surmised. He'd advised Isobel to contact the local GP and acquaint him with the circumstances of her mother's condition. He just hoped the old lady wasn't suffering a relapse. He couldn't help thinking she'd have been better off back in town.

And yet he could understand her love of this area. Wasn't he already speculating on the possibilities of working here in future and only going into the office when it was absolutely necessary? One of the advantages of his profession was that he could work virtually anywhere, so long as he had a computer, and as he seldom went anywhere without his laptop there was no problem.

Of course, he thought, as he went up the steps to the front door, the laptop would only be a temporary measure. He'd ask Isobel to allocate him one of the unused guest rooms and he'd set up a bank of equipment in there. It was time he gave Shane more responsibility. Time he started enjoying more of the success that had cost him so dearly.

The doors were open and somewhere he could hear the sound of an electric drill. The smell of paint was more pervasive this morning and he guessed Andy's contractors were hard at work. It pleased him that the house was beginning to feel more and more as it used to. More and more like a home....

He had barely stepped inside when Isobel appeared. He noticed she had changed into a skirt and blouse and her hair was now confined in its usual knot at her nape. It pleased him that only a couple of hours earlier it had been spread across his pillows, and his mouth took on a frankly sensual curve.

He was picturing her as he'd seen her last, and he wondered if that was why she suddenly looked so apprehensive. Was she remembering it, too? Had she any idea how desirable she looked with that guilty flush staining her cheeks and her tongue peeping sensuously between her lips? Somehow he doubted it.

Dear God, he was getting hard again. Indeed, ever since

he'd come out of the shower he'd been in a semi-aroused state, and he wondered if there was any chance of him spiriting her away from here for a while, so that they could be alone.

But before he could say anything Isobel forestalled him. 'Did you forget something?' she asked, her clipped tone immediately dousing his excitement. 'If you've brought the money back—'

'I haven't.' Jake took a couple of steps towards her and then halted as she withdrew the same number of paces. He sighed. 'I think we need to talk.'

'I don't think so.' She was absurdly emphatic. 'I don't think we have anything to say to one another. You want a divorce? Fine. Just get your solicitor to contact mine. I don't believe there's any reason why we should meet again.'

Jake was stunned. 'You don't understand—' he began, but she wouldn't let him go on.

'Oh, I think I do,' she said harshly. 'This morning was your attempt to show me what I'd lost and you succeeded.'

'No—'

'Whatever.' She waved a careless hand. 'It should never have happened, and wouldn't have if I hadn't been stupid enough to trust you. I thought you'd understand how I felt about the money, not expect me to pay in kind. Well, you've had your pound of flesh but, guess what? It was a freebie! I don't want anything from you but your assurance that you won't penalise Emily or my mother for my frailties.'

Jake stared at her incredulously. 'Is that what you really think?' he demanded. 'That what happened was some pathetic attempt on my part to exact revenge?'

'Well, wasn't it?'

'No, dammit, it wasn't.'

'But you know it should never have happened?'

'Why not?'

'Why not?' He saw the convulsive swallow that rippled down her throat. 'You know why not. Or are you as indifferent to Ms Duncan's feelings as you were to mine?'

Jake swore. 'Marcie doesn't come into this.'

'Doesn't she?' Isobel looked scornful now. 'I thought you were going to marry her.'

Well, I'm not.

The words trembled on his tongue, but before he could bring himself to say them he heard a sound at the top of the stairs. A man was coming out of the room he knew belonged to Isobel's mother and his jaw compressed impatiently. The doctor, he thought, resenting the interruption. And, judging by the sound of raised voices, Lady Hannah had been as pleased to see him as he was. He couldn't make out what she was saying but Emily, who came running down the stairs ahead of the man, was upset, and that irritated him no end.

'Mummy, Mummy,' she was crying tearfully. Then she saw Jake. At once her eyes widened and her fingers came to knuckle the tears from her cheeks. And, to his astonishment, instead of running to her mother, she rushed towards him, wrapping her arms around his waist and burying her face against his sweater.

'Hey, hey.' Jake didn't want to feel such an instinctive empathy with her, but it seemed to well up from deep inside him and he couldn't deny it. 'Emily; Em! What's the matter? What did the doctor say?'

'The doctor?' Emily tipped her head back and looked up at him with puzzled eyes. 'What doctor?'

'I assume you mean me,' remarked the drawling tones of the man Jake had hoped never to have to see again. 'Hello, McCabe. Long time, no see.'

Jake's fingers briefly tightened on Emily's shoulders. But then, with careful deliberation, he put her away from him.

'Mallory,' he said coldly. 'Still making women cry, see.'

'Oh, I wouldn't say that.' Piers was remarkably cool, onsidering the last time they'd met Jake had almost beaten im to a pulp. He looked from Jake to Isobel and back gain. 'I'd say it's a toss-up which of us your wife least vants to see.'

Jake was tempted to tell him he was wrong. He doubted iers would be standing there with such a smug look on is face if he knew that only a couple of hours ago Jake nd Isobel had been locked in a hot and sweaty embrace 1 Jake's hotel room. He'd have loved to describe exactly vhat they'd been doing in great detail, how very pleasur- ble and satisfying it had been. But he couldn't do it.

Apart from anything else, he couldn't expose such inti- nacies in front of the child. Besides, after what Isobel had ist been saying, his own interpretation of events had suf- ered a severe setback. He'd really believed she'd wanted im, that what they'd shared had been a spiritual as well s a physical experience. Surely they'd shared their souls, ot just their bodies?

But now he didn't know what to think. Piers was here, or the second time in two days, if Emily was to be be- eved, and he had no reason to doubt her. Isobel's behav- our took on a whole new aspect in light of that revelation.

Isobel apparently had no such reservations. 'I think you nould leave,' she said. 'Both of you. I don't want you ere.'

'Belle!'

Jake couldn't prevent the involuntary protest, and Emily gged at her mother's sleeve with protesting fingers. But obel was adamant.

'Must I remind you that there's a sick woman upstairs? don't know what you've been saying to her—' this to

Piers '—but it's obvious you've upset her and I want you to go.'

'Oh, Issie…' Piers had always irritated Jake with his pet name for her and it wasn't any different now. 'You know you don't mean that.'

'I do.' As Jake watched with disbelieving eyes, she gestured towards the door. 'I told you yesterday that you weren't welcome here. Now, must I get one of the workmen to throw you out?'

'Why do I know you'd never do that?' Piers mocked gently. 'Issie, we both know how your mother would feel if you embarrassed her like that.'

'Let me do it.' The words were out before Jake could prevent them. He'd never seen Piers in this light before, and the knowledge disturbed him. His eyes narrowed on the man he had once thought was his friend. 'You've no idea how much pleasure it would give me.'

'The only pleasure you're likely to get from this relationship, eh, McCabe?' taunted Piers, unaware of the thin line he was walking. He turned back to Isobel. 'As far as what I've been saying to your mother, Issie, perhaps you ought to ask her that question. I doubt you'll get an answer, though. You never did before.'

'What's that supposed to mean?'

Isobel was confused and Jake stepped forward. 'Don' you see what he's doing, Belle?' he demanded harshly 'He's trying to drive a rift between you and your mother just as he drove a rift between us. I didn't believe it before but now—'

'Oh, but that was a much more pleasurable rift,' mocked Piers, clearly wanting to provoke him. 'Did I ever tell you how eager she was? How hot and sexy? She couldn't wai to get into my bed. She was itching for it—'

'That's not true!'

Jake's fist was arrested by a frail aristocratic voice and

urning, he saw Lady Hannah clinging to the banister halfway down the stairs.

'Don't touch him, Jake,' she implored. 'Don't give him
any reason to do any more damage to this family than he
has already done.'

'Mama?' It was Isobel who spoke, before rushing up the
stairs to grasp her mother's arm. 'Mama, you shouldn't be
out of bed!'

'Chickens coming home to roost, eh, Lady Hannah?'
Piers jeered, and Jake couldn't prevent his hand from shooting out and fastening on the collar of Mallory's jacket.

'I think we've heard enough from you,' he said, amazed
at the satisfaction he got at seeing Piers's reaction. However
rocky the other man might pretend to be, he wasn't totally
indifferent to the threat Jake offered. 'Come on. You're
leaving.'

'Not yet.' Despite her daughter's efforts to get her to go
back upstairs, Lady Hannah hadn't finished what she had
to say. 'Listen to me, Jake. Piers never seduced your wife.
That was my doing.'

'What?'

'What are you saying, Mama?'

It was difficult to tell which of them was the most
shocked by her confession, and, predictably, it was Piers
who recovered first.

Dragging himself away from Jake's unresisting hand, he
straightened his collar before saying contemptuously, 'Now
I've heard everything.' He looked up at the old lady with
scornful eyes. 'What you'll do to keep this old ruin from
falling about your ears! What are you saying? That you
seduced your daughter yourself?'

'Don't—don't you dare say such filthy things to me.'
Lady Hannah swayed and Isobel had a struggle to keep her
upright. 'You know I'm telling the truth. I told you to get

into bed with Isobel when I heard Jake's car coming up the
drive.'

'What?'

Isobel stared at her mother now, as if she'd never seen
her before, and Jake struggled to make sense of what the
old woman was saying. It couldn't be true. Lady Hannah
couldn't have accomplished such a thing on her own. What
about Isobel? Isobel must have been a willing accomplice
however shocked she appeared now.

'It's true,' said the old lady weakly. 'Oh, I'm not denying
it was what I'd been angling for. I never wanted Isobel to
marry you. I never thought you were good enough for her.
But she wouldn't look at Piers, even though he'd loved her
for years.'

'Mama!'

Lady Hannah shook her head. 'I know it was wrong now,
but it seemed a good idea at the time. And getting you to
Mattingley was easy enough. I knew you wouldn't let me
come up on my own and I saw my chance.'

'Oh, Mama.'

Isobel's voice was breaking now, and Piers seemed to
see a chance to intervene. 'Don't pretend you didn't know
what was happening,' he sneered. 'You were hungry for
it.'

'No—'

Jake didn't know if Isobel's cry was a plaintive denial
or a plea to him not to act on Piers's ugly words. Whatever,
this time it came too late to prevent the inevitable, and his
fist smashed heavily into Mallory's face. His knuckles
stung, but not as much as Piers's nose, he'd bet, and as
blood sprayed hotly over the collar of his shirt Emily burst
into tears.

Until that moment he'd forgotten the child was there, but
now he pulled her into his arms, comforting her with little
words of reassurance as he rubbed her trembling shoulders.

'It's okay, it's okay, sweetheart,' he said, over and over, while Piers struggled to douse the blood streaming from his nose with his handkerchief.

But Isobel wasn't finished.

'You—you got me drunk,' she said, as if remembering the circumstances of the event. She groaned. 'Oh, God, you got me drunk! You *wanted* Piers to seduce me. That was your plan all along.'

Lady Hannah lifted a trembling hand. 'I was a fool. I've told you. I know that now.' She drew a laboured breath. 'Can you ever forgive me?'

'You didn't think that I might be pregnant.' Isobel choked on the words. 'You didn't consider my feelings at all. All you ever think about is this house, as Piers said.'

'That may have been true once, Isobel, but not now.' Her mother was desperate; Jake could see that. 'Please, believe me.'

But, as Isobel brushed her mother's pleas aside and stumbled down the stairs, his own emotions were suddenly shattered by the realisation of what this meant to him. Dear God, Emily was his daughter. All these years, when he'd been denying her existence, she'd been growing up without her father's support.

'Belle,' he said, reaching out a hand as Isobel went past him, but she barely looked at him.

'Don't touch me,' she said, in a strained voice. 'Don't any of you touch me. You're all as bad as each other.'

'Belle!' Jake was desperate now. 'I didn't know. I didn't know what to think.'

'You didn't believe me,' she said, her eyes as clear and cold as an arctic lake. 'Do you think this makes a difference? Do you honestly think because my mother has absolved me of all blame that I'll forgive you for what you've done? That I'll forgive any of you? Grow up, Jake. I don't need your absolution. I don't need anything any more.'

And, without another word, she marched out through the
front door. But it wasn't until he heard the sound of the
Porsche accelerating down the drive that he remembered
he'd left his keys in the ignition.

CHAPTER TWELVE

'DADDY, Granny says there's a fly buzzing round the room and it's driving her mad. Can you come and get it?'

Jake heaved a sigh. He knew he should be used to Lady Hannah's antics by now, but, despite the fact that he was sure the fly would have miraculously disappeared by the time he got to the old lady's apartments, he obediently got up from the computer and accompanied his daughter along the corridor to her room.

'You don't mind, do you, Daddy?' Emily asked anxiously, and Jake found a smile for her benefit.

''Course not,' he said, putting his arm around the child's narrow shoulders and giving a squeeze. It was a relief to see that Emily seemed to be recovering from her distress her mother's disappearance at last. Somehow Jake had managed to convince her that Isobel would come back when she was ready, and apparently Emily was adapting to that eventuality.

Nevertheless, it had been a long three weeks since Isobel had driven off in the Porsche. To begin with Emily had been inconsolable, and Jake knew it had to be an indication of Isobel's state of mind that she'd abandoned her daughter like that. He had had his work cut out just comforting the child. And Lady Hannah hadn't been much better. She'd blamed herself—with good reason—and Jake had given up any thought of returning to London until Isobel got back. If she got back. But Jake refused to consider that possibility.

'Mrs Edwards says it's cottage pie for supper,' offered Emily suddenly. 'Granny likes that.'

'Sounds good.' Jake was upbeat, but in all honesty h couldn't have cared less. His appetite was virtually no existent. 'What do you think?'

'It's okay.' Emily was indifferent. Clearly she had som thing else on her mind. Then, with endearing honesty, sl said, 'I wish Mummy would come back.'

Don't we all? thought Jake, but he deliberately put on cheerful face. 'She'll be back soon,' he said. 'Like I to you: she just needs a little time to be on her own, that all. She knew I'd stay here and look after you and Granny

'Did she?'

Emily didn't sound convinced, and Jake had to admit wasn't a situation he would have visualised his wife pe mitting in the normal way. But then, when Isobel had le Mattingley she'd behaved anything but normally, and was this more than anything that had persuaded him to ale the police to her disappearance.

He'd kept it low key, of course. He hadn't wanted squad car screaming up to the doors of Mattingley and posse of police officers swarming all over the propert He'd merely had a word with the Assistant Chief Constab and explained a little of the circumstances surroundi Isobel's departure to him. In consequence, a covert inve tigation had been made. Unfortunately, without any po tive results.

The possibility that she might have done some injury herself was a constant nightmare. No one knew better th Jake how disastrous betrayal could feel, and the Porsc was a powerful vehicle on which to vent your grief. Imag of her losing control on one of the treacherous bends th littered these moors or plunging into a water-filled quar tormented him. He knew the police had checked the clif that edged the coastline. There was always the fear that s had driven the car over the cliffs and been swept c to sea.

The fact that nothing had been found was little consolation. People disappeared every day and were never seen again. His only real hope was that Isobel wouldn't do that to Emily.

'Are you cross because I interrupted you?' Emily asked suddenly, and Jake realised she had mistaken his silence for annoyance.

'How could I be cross with you?' he exclaimed, giving her another hug. 'We're pals, aren't we? We don't have to stand on ceremony with one another.'

'And you don't mind staying here?' she persisted, and he sighed.

'Of course I don't. It's given us a chance to get to know one another properly.'

'And you really do believe that I'm your daughter now, don't you?' Emily asked with some satisfaction, and Jake realised that if nothing else it had brought them closer together.

'No question,' he assured her with another squeeze. 'I can't imagine why I had any doubts.'

'But you did?'

'I made a mistake,' said Jake gently. 'A terrible mistake. I believed someone else.'

'Mr Mallory?'

Emily was sharp. Jake would give her that.

'It doesn't matter now,' he said, wondering if Isobel knew or even cared how bittersweet that knowledge was. Of course, she must have known he'd take care of Emily, whatever happened. Otherwise she would never have left her with him. Perhaps she'd thought he'd return to London and take Emily to his home. After all, she still believed he was going to marry Marcie.

Isobel's mother was propped up on her pillows when he entered the bedroom. She looked frailer than ever and, despite the fact that he had nothing to thank her for, Jake found he couldn't hate her. She'd done what she'd done for her own reasons, but there was no doubt that in the last three weeks she'd paid for it.

He'd never known his own mother, of course, but he knew that if she'd behaved towards him as Lady Hannah had Isobel, he'd have felt completely different. Isobel was her own flesh and blood. Was any house worth such a sacrifice?

'Oh, Jake,' she said now, when he came in with her granddaughter. 'I'm sorry to disturb you, but there's been a fly buzzing at the windows for the past hour.'

Jake nodded. 'So I hear.' He crossed the room and scanned the glass. 'Where is it?'

'Isn't it there?' Lady Hannah sounded anxious, and Jake gave a resigned sigh.

'It doesn't look like it,' he said tolerantly. 'It must have followed Emily out.'

'Oh, yes.' The old lady jumped on the explanation, proving that, as Jake had anticipated, there'd been no fly in the first place. 'Oh, well, as you're here now, perhaps you'd like to join me in a cup of tea?'

Jake hesitated. He saw the tray of tea now, cooling on the bedside table, and guessed this had been her plan all along.

'Well—'

'I know you're busy, and I know that working here can't be very satisfactory for you, particularly as we've taken up so much of your time, but I wish you would stay for a few minutes. I want to talk to you.'

It was the longest speech the old lady had made since Isobel's departure and she was breathless at the end of it. So breathless, in fact, that Jake felt obliged to pull the tapestry-covered bedside chair towards the bed and drop into it. 'Okay,' he said. 'Shall I pour?'

'Oh, would you?' Lady Hannah managed a faint smile.

Then she turned to her granddaughter. 'I'm afraid I don't have any orange juice, Emily. Perhaps you'd run down to Mrs Edwards and ask her for a glass.'

'I don't want any orange juice,' said Emily at once, propping her hip against the back of her father's chair. 'I'm not thirsty.'

Her grandmother's lips tightened, but before the old lady could say anything to upset the child Jake intervened. 'I think your granny means she wants to have a private word with me,' he said, twisting his head to look up at her. 'Why don't you go and check out the game I've just installed on the laptop? It's a totally new concept called Predators. I'd be interested to hear what you think of it.'

'Really?' Emily was incredulous. 'I can use your computer?'

'So long as you don't try and access my files,' remarked Jake drily. 'Yeah, go on. I was going to show it to you later anyway.'

'Cool.'

Her anxieties forgotten, Emily darted out of the room, and Lady Hannah bestowed a grateful look on her son-in-law. 'Thank you.'

'Hey, I didn't do it for you,' Jake responded, making no attempt to pour the tea. 'What do you want?'

'So direct,' said Lady Hannah with a bitter smile. 'And you wondered why I didn't want Isobel to marry you.'

Jake shook his head. 'I never wondered that, old lady. What you really mean is that I didn't have enough class for your daughter. Well, okay. I'll give you that. But I can't believe you think she'd have been happier with that two-faced bastard I used to call my friend.'

'No...' She gave him that, plucking at the bedspread with fingers that were now as thin and brittle as talons. 'I was wrong about that, as I've been about so many things. That's why I want to try and put them right.'

'Oh, yeah?' Jake was suspicious. 'What did you have in mind?'

Lady Hannah hesitated. 'I'm going to alter my will.' She moistened her dry lips. 'I'm going to leave Mattingley to you.'

'No!' Jake had pushed the chair back and was on his feet almost before she'd finished speaking. 'You're crazy!'

'No, I'm not.' Lady Hannah's voice was gaining strength again. 'This place can only be an albatross around Isobel's neck. It's mortgaged to the hilt, as you know, and the death duties alone will be crippling. You can afford it. Isobel can't. But I want it to stay in the family. I want Emily to continue to be able to come here, to know her heritage. If I leave it to Isobel it will be sold and that will be that.'

'If she comes back,' said Jake savagely, not caring in that moment if he upset her or not. What she was suggesting was cruel, barbaric. The selfish judgement of a woman who cared for little beyond her own vainglorious ends.

At least his words had the effect he'd hoped for. 'What do you mean?' she demanded, her face leached of all colour. 'What have you heard?'

'I've heard nothing,' retorted Jake, slamming the chair aside and striding restlessly about the room. 'But dammit, woman, have you no shame?'

Lady Hannah held up her head. 'I don't think you have any room to criticise me, Jake,' she declared, a tremor in her voice. She gestured in the direction Emily had taken. 'For the past ten years you've denied that little girl's existence.'

'And whose fault was that?'

'Not mine,' said his mother-in-law doggedly. 'You did that all by yourself.'

Jake scowled. 'I don't understand you. You were willing to take my money but you were afraid that we might get back together. Why? I've often wondered. Why?'

'Then you're not half as astute as I thought,' declared
the old lady scornfully. 'Think about it. Do you honestly
believe I wanted you to find out that Emily was yours?'

Jake stared at her uncomprehendingly for a moment.
What the hell was she talking about? And then, like a streak
of lightning, understanding dawned. '*You* didn't want to be
found out,' he accused her incredulously. 'My God, you let
me go on thinking Isobel had betrayed me because you
couldn't face what would happen if she found out how
you'd tried to manipulate her.'

Lady Hannah's features looked shrunken now. 'You
have such an elegant way of putting it,' she said tightly.
'But, in essence, yes. That is what I thought.'

Jake shook his head. 'I guess you hoped that if I wasn't
around Isobel might begin to see Mallory in a different
light. Oh, boy, that must have been some disappointment.'

'I didn't know she was pregnant, did I?' retorted the old
woman bitterly. 'If I'd had any hopes in that direction they
were shattered when Isobel's condition became too obvious
to ignore.'

'And Mallory knew the baby couldn't be his,' exclaimed
Jake triumphantly. 'My God, I used to wonder why Piers
never attempted to see his daughter. Why Isobel insisted
she never wanted to see him again.'

'You weren't interested enough to do anything about it,'
pointed out his mother-in-law tartly. 'We've neither of us
come out of this untarnished, Jake. We both have our
crosses to bear.'

Which was nothing but the truth, he thought, even if he
didn't want to believe it. Yet, he consoled himself, he
hadn't instigated what had happened. Lady Hannah had.
And now she wanted to compound the offence by leaving
Mattingley to him.

'I don't want the house,' he said, pushing his thumbs

into the waistband at the back of his pants. 'I won't accept it. Mattingley belongs to the Laceys, not the McCabes.'

'But you could do so much with it,' cried the old lady desperately. 'You have the money. You could restore it to its former glory. I realise Ms Duncan may not want to live here, but at weekends—'

'I'm not going to marry Marcie Duncan,' declared Jake flatly, voicing the decision he'd made the morning Isobel had come to the pub to see him. 'I told her when she got back from Jamaica. She's presently deciding whether she's going to sue me for breach of promise or accept the settlement I've offered her. I've pointed out that, as I'm still married to Isobel, it might be difficult proving breach of promise, but she's got to decide for herself.'

Lady Hannah's lips twitched. 'You are a bastard, Jake,' she said, not without some admiration, and he shrugged.

'So they tell me,' he said, heading for the door. 'So— no more talk about changing your will, eh?'

'I may not need to,' murmured his nemesis smugly, and Jake frowned.

'What do you mean?'

Lady Hannah considered. 'Well, if you're not going to marry Ms Duncan, I can only assume that that's because you still care about Isobel. Who knows? Now that the truth is out, you two may get back together.'

Jake shook his head. 'I wouldn't hold your breath.'

Lady Hannah bit her lip. 'She still cares about you, you know. Nothing I say can change that.'

'And you're still manipulating,' retorted Jake, reaching the door. 'Drink your tea. I've got work to do.'

CHAPTER THIRTEEN

IT WAS almost light when Isobel drove into the village. She'd driven all night to avoid the traffic and any vigilant policeman or woman who might be looking out for the car. She had no doubt that Jake would have reported her missing. She just hoped he hadn't frightened Emily by telling her scary stories about why her mother had abandoned her as she had.

And she *had* abandoned her daughter. Or rather, she'd needed to get away from Jake and her mother and Piers and Emily had been caught in the middle. There'd been no way she could have taken the child with her. After learning that he really was Emily's father, Jake would never have allowed her to abduct her as well.

Well, abduction was rather an emotive word, she acknowledged wearily, the strain of driving for several hours without a break beginning to take its toll. Besides, however she might resent it, Jake needed time to get to know his daughter, for her sake. Time to introduce her to her new stepmother-to-be.

She was assuming Jake would have taken Emily back to London with him. It was over three weeks since she'd taken off with his Porsche and there was no way he could have neglected his business for so long. She knew Emily wasn't back at school, but that was no surprise, really. Jake would be doing everything he could to make up for all the years he'd denied her existence.

As far as Lady Hannah was concerned Isobel did feel some remorse, but generally she'd found it better not to think about her mother at all. She didn't want to feel sorry for her, didn't want to feel any sympathy for the state she was in. The woman had lied to her. Not just about the money she'd been accepting from Jake on a regular basis, but about the most fundamental issue of her life.

She had deliberately—and maliciously—destroyed her daughter's marriage. Even when Emily was born she'd done nothing to betray her own hand in the events of the past year. Mattingley meant more to her than her own daughter's happiness. Isobel couldn't forget that, and forgiveness seemed very far away.

She stopped at the gates and endeavoured to calm herself before continuing. A glance at her watch told her it was barely six o'clock, and she doubted anyone would be up at this hour. She felt a twinge of guilt at leaving Mrs Edwards to cope with her mother single-handed. But, knowing Jake, he'd probably have arranged for nursing care before he went back to town.

He was like that, she thought unhappily, resting her aching head on the steering wheel. However unforgiving he had been towards her, he'd always showed compassion towards Lady Hannah. Not that she'd known about that either.

Pressing her foot on the accelerator, she drove on, only to slow in surprise at the sight of hedges newly trimmed and lawns newly mown. The pond didn't look much different, but there were lilies growing in the reeds now, and stocks and azaleas making a colourful display between the trees.

Someone had been busy, she reflected, and she doubted Mr Edwards had accomplished this all on his own. Jake must have hired a firm of landscape gardeners, too, she guessed, before he left. He had certainly gone to a lot of trouble for a house that was going to be sold as soon as—

But she didn't finish the sentence. However bitter she felt towards her mother, she didn't wish the old lady dead.

ndeed, she knew that in spite of everything Lady Hannah's departure would leave a distinct hole in her life. Particularly now that Emily was obviously going to want to spend some of her time with her father. It didn't take a genius to figure out that Jake would soon realise, as she had, how much like he and Emily were.

Slowing as she reached the turnaround in front of the house, Isobel brought the car to a halt and turned off the ignition. Then she sat for a moment, admiring the containers of geraniums and impatiens that were set at either side of the heavy door. Although the outside of the house hadn't been painted, it had definitely lost its air of neglect. Her mother must be delighted, she thought, not without a touch of poignancy. This was what Lady Hannah had always wanted.

Isobel had no luggage to unload from the car. Just the simple shoulder bag Sarah had provided to hold the few cosmetics and little money she had given her. It had proved an unnecessary kindness. Isobel hadn't spent any money and she hadn't worn any make-up for weeks. But then, she hadn't left the Danielses house since she'd arrived there, red-eyed and desperate, three weeks ago.

Sarah and her husband, Ross, had proved to be good friends. Even though Isobel had told them little of what had happened, they hadn't asked any questions, simply giving her a room, a garage to hide the car, and the time she needed to heal.

When she'd decided to leave, they hadn't tried to change her mind. Ross had taken the car to a petrol station and filled the Porsche's tank for her, and she had promised to ring them as soon as she got to Mattingley. That was what she intended to do. Just as soon as she'd made herself a cup of coffee…

She closed the car door without slamming it, pocketing the keys as she walked towards the house. The tight denim jeans and cropped tee shirt were Sarah's, too, and she'd worn them deliberately, knowing her mother would deplore such clothes. But her mother's opinion no longer mattered to her. She was not looking forward to facing the woman who had so selfishly ruined her life.

She walked round to the back of the building, hoping the kitchen door would be unlocked. It often was. The apartments the Edwardses occupied were accessed via a passageway that opened off the kitchen, and Mrs Edwards invariably forgot to lock the outer door.

As she'd expected, the handle of the boot room door turned easily, and she stepped quietly into the muddle of Wellington boots and outdoor shoes that littered the floor. No change there, then, she mused wryly, before opening the door into the kitchen itself.

It was like *déjà vu*, only this time Jake was fully clothed. He was standing with his hips propped against the counter beside the sink, arms folded across his chest, fingers tucked beneath his arms. He appeared to be lost in thought, and Isobel assumed at first he hadn't heard her. But then his head turned, and if she'd had any idea of withdrawing again it was swiftly banished by the disbelieving anguish in his face.

'Belle?' he said faintly, almost as if he believed he was hallucinating. His arms dropped to his sides. 'God, Belle, is that really you?'

'Really me,' she echoed, her voice as thready as his. She came into the room and closed the door behind her, leaning back against it, glad of its support. 'What are you doing here?'

Jake shook his head, and as he did so Isobel saw the pot of coffee percolating on the stove. In her absence someone—Jake?—had provided a proper coffee-maker, and the smell of the ground beans was tantalisingly familiar.

Realising he must have been waiting for the coffee to

brew, Isobel wondered if the jolt of excitement she'd felt at finding him there was premature. What if Marcie was here, too? Anything was possible. It was Saturday morning, after all.

Deciding there was only one way to find out, she didn't give him time to answer her question before saying lightly, 'That smells good. May I have some?'

Jake blew out a breath. 'Is that all you have to say?' he demanded, and now she heard the underlying note of anger in his voice. 'Where the hell have you been?'

Isobel held up her head. 'I don't think that's any business of yours,' she said, resenting his proprietary attitude, and Jake scowled.

'The hell it's not,' he snapped, raking his fingers through his hair and leaving gold-streaked silver strands sticking out in all directions. 'Do you have any idea how worried we've been about you?'

Isobel straightened her spine. 'There was no need—'

'No need?' Jake took two steps towards her and then halted, as if he didn't trust himself to get any nearer without shaking her. 'Dammit, Belle, where have you been? I've been nearly out of my mind.'

Isobel lifted her shoulders in a nervous gesture, not quite knowing how to answer him. Was this resentment she was hearing, or real concern? Where was Emily? Where had she spent the last three weeks? Surely Jake hadn't left her here, with two old people and a dying woman?

'I—needed some time to think,' she said at last, deciding he deserved some explanation. Then, moistening her lips, 'Where's Emily? I have to tell her I'm back.'

'Presently.' Jake stepped between her and the hall door, and she knew there was no way she was going to get out of the kitchen without telling him what she'd been doing for the past three weeks. 'I want to know where you've been staying. Not in this area, I'll bet. The police have combed every inch of these moors looking for you.'

'The police!' Isobel was horrified. 'There was no need to involve the police.'

'Wasn't there?' Jake glared at her angrily. 'When you left here no one knew what the hell you were going to do. And you're not used to driving the Porsche. That was something else I had to think about. The Range Rover is fine, but it doesn't have the Porsche's acceleration.'

'Oh, right.' Isobel felt bitter. 'You were concerned about your car. Well, don't worry, Jake, it's still in one piece. It's been sitting in a friend's lock-up in Kensington for the past three weeks.'

Jake swore then. 'I don't give a damn about the car,' he told her savagely. 'It's you I was worried about. God, I was beginning to fear the worst.'

Isobel felt a little guilty now. 'Well, as I say, there was no need for you to concern yourself,' she declared defensively. 'I realised that Emily might worry, and I was sorry about that, but I had to get away. I've been staying with a friend, Sarah. I knew—I hoped—that you'd look after Emily for me.' She glanced beyond him. 'Is she upstairs?'

'Where else would she be?' demanded Jake explosively. 'Like me, she's had to stay and face the situation. She didn't have the luxury of anywhere else to go.'

Isobel blinked. 'But—didn't you take her back to London?'

'To London?' Jake looked perplexed now. 'Why would I take her to London?'

Isobel blinked. 'Well—I assumed you left just after me.'

'No.'

'What do you mean, no?'

'I mean, I haven't been anywhere,' retorted Jake, his jaw compressing tensely. 'Except to get my things from the pub, of course. I hope you don't mind. I moved back into the house.'

Isobel was stunned. 'But I don't understand—'

'No.' Jake seemed to accept that assessment. 'You don't.'

Isobel tried to make sense of what he was saying. 'So— you've been here for—for—'

'For the past three weeks, yes.'

'You haven't been back to London?'

'No.'

She swallowed. 'Then—then is—is Ms Duncan here, too?'

Jake's face twisted in disbelief. 'Oh, yeah, right,' he said harshly. 'I'd do that, wouldn't I? Bring another woman into my wife's house? It's the sort of thing you'd expect me to do, is it? Rub Emily's nose in it by bringing Marcie here?'

Isobel drew a breath. 'I don't know what you're capable of, do I? For a man who professes to love one woman, you seem to have an inordinate interest in another.'

'You being the other?' suggested Jake tightly. 'But then, that shouldn't surprise you. You always could get under my skin.'

As you can get under mine, thought Isobel painfully, wishing she knew what was going on. What was Jake doing here? Had he only stayed because of Emily? And, if so, why hadn't he made other arrangements? Emily would have loved going to London with him and staying at his house.

'Please…' she said, feeling inordinately tired suddenly. 'I've been driving all night. Do you think I could have a cup of coffee before we go on? I realise I've misjudged you, and I'm grateful if you've stayed on Emily's account.' She hesitated. 'And—and my mother's. H-how is Lady Hannah? I suppose I have to ask.'

Jake grabbed a mug, filled it with some of the aromatic

liquid and pushed it towards her. 'Here,' he said, without much ceremony. 'You look as though you need it. You've hardly got an ounce of colour in your face.'

'Thanks.'

Isobel lifted the mug in both hands and attempted to take a sip. But her hands were shaking and some dribbled down her chin. Then, when she freed one hand to wipe her face, the hot mug burned the other, and, jerking back automatically, she sent coffee flying everywhere.

Some splashed onto Jake's arm as he came forward instinctively to help her, and he uttered an impatient oath before wresting the mug out of her unresisting hand.

'It's okay,' he said as she cowered back, covering her cheeks with her spread fingers. 'Accidents happen,' he added, seeming to sense that she was at the end of her tether. 'Come on, baby. Relax. You're among friends here.'

'Am I?' Isobel looked up at him through her lashes, and Jake thrust the mug aside and pulled her into his arms.

'What do you think?' he said thickly, pressing her face against his shoulder. 'God, Belle, you can't know how glad I am to see you. I was beginning to wonder if you were ever going to come back.'

'And that mattered?' she whispered huskily, knowing she was going to regret asking that question when she was in such an emotive state, but it was too late now.

'It mattered,' he assured her, his fingers moving in her hair. 'We've all been worried sick about you. However despicably the old girl upstairs behaved, she loves you. You must never doubt that.'

'In her own way,' said Isobel in a muffled voice, realising she was reading much too much into the embrace. Besides which, she still hadn't forgiven Jake for not believing in her all these years. Okay, so her mother had deceived him, too, but he should have had more faith in her.

Yet would she, in his position? If she'd come upon him and—Marcie, say—in his bed, wouldn't she have believed the worst if Marcie said she was pregnant? She rather thought so.

'I—I'd better go up and tell Emily I'm back,' she said now, making a belated effort to rescue the situation. It wouldn't do for Jake to think she wanted a repeat of that morning in his hotel room. She had to accept the fact that Jake would always have some lingering attraction to her. But it wasn't fair for her to act upon it, not when his emotions had not been stirred by passion, but relief.

Ironically, Jake didn't seem to want to let her go. When she tried to step back from him he moved, so that she was between him and the counter, the hard edge of the steel drainer digging into her back.

'Not yet,' he said, his voice thickening as his eyes dropped to her mouth. The look he bestowed upon her was almost tangible, and the sweet anticipation of what he was thinking caused a weakness in her legs.

'Jake—' She felt the dryness in her mouth and swallowed convulsively. 'This isn't a good idea.'

'It's the only idea I've got,' he muttered, taking her face between his hands and staring down at her hungrily. 'For Em's sake, Belle, have a little pity. We can't let one old woman's selfishness ruin the rest of our lives.'

Isobel quivered. Although he was cupping her face in his hands, his body was resting against hers, and she was not indifferent to the fact that he was becoming aroused. His manhood was hard and pulsing with desire, his thigh wedged between hers inflaming the dampening core between her legs. He wanted to make love to her. He was making no secret of the fact. And she wanted it, too. Right here, right now; on the draining board, if necessary. Just so long as he satisfied the ache that refused to go away.

'Jake—'

She tried to make one plea to his better nature, but he wasn't listening to her. Bending his head, he covered her trembling mouth with his. She inhaled raggedly as his lips bled fire into her senses, and against all the advice she'd given herself these past weeks she tilted her head and wound her arms around his neck.

It was heaven and it was hell. Heaven because this was what she really wanted, where she really wanted to be. And hell because she knew it was wrong. She couldn't be his part-time lover. Whatever self-respect she had left would soon vanish if she allowed him to use her as and when he felt the need.

His hand was on her breast now, sliding beneath the conveniently short hem of the tee shirt, unfastening her bra and letting her flesh swell against his palm. Her nipples were hard, achingly sensitive. Whatever message her body was getting, it wasn't the one she was sending from her brain.

'God, you drive me crazy,' he muttered, his hands skimming down her spine to the rounded curve of her hip. With obvious deliberation he pressed her against him, rotating his hips against hers, making her dizzily aware of how this was going to end.

'Jake—I can't do this,' she moaned, before her body betrayed her completely, and Jake drew back only far enough to rest his forehead against hers.

'It's what you want,' he said in an anguished voice. 'It's what we both want.'

'I know,' she whispered brokenly. 'But I can't be a substitute for Marcie. I realise you've not seen her for several weeks, and you're—you're—'

'Horny?' he asked huskily, a trace of humour lifting his lips, and she blinked away the tears that threatened at this evidence of his duplicity.

'Yes,' she said staunchly, prepared to make a fight of it

if she had to. But Jake only stared into her eyes and said steadily, 'I don't want a divorce.'

Isobel was confused. What did he mean? That he was going to remain married to her—for Emily's sake, perhaps?—and keep the other woman on the side?'

'I don't—'

'Marcie and I are finished,' Jake told her softly. 'I came to tell you that the morning I found Mallory in the house. Since then, what with Emily's tears and Lady Hannah's revelations, not to mention the disappearing act you put on, I haven't had a chance to explain.'

'But—' Isobel tried to think. 'What about Emily?'

'What about Emily?'

'Well, you didn't believe she was your daughter then, did you?'

'No.' Jake conceded the fact with a rueful sigh. 'But I'd already decided that I wanted you too much to make Em the scapegoat for my frustrations. As far as I was concerned she was your daughter. That was going to have to be enough.'

Isobel stared up at him. 'Do you mean that?' she asked tremulously, and Jake rubbed his lips against her cheek.

'The question is, do you want me to mean it?' he asked gently. 'I know I've behaved pretty abominably, but I'm hoping you love me enough to forgive me.'

Isobel caught her breath, one hand curving along his jaw, where the roughness of overnight stubble was probably again leaving its mark on her skin. 'I forgive you,' she said. 'And I love you. But you know that. You've always known that. I never wanted us to separate in the first place.'

'No.' Jake was contrite. 'I was a fool.'

'No, you were human,' said Isobel honestly. 'In your position, I'd probably have felt exactly the same.'

Jake's lips brushed hers once, twice, then clung, heating

her blood as her arms crept eagerly about his waist. Dear God, she thought, she'd anticipated many things during her journey up the motorway, but in her wildest dreams she'd never imagined anything as wonderful as this.

CHAPTER FOURTEEN

JAKE'S kiss deepened, hardened, lengthened, the urgency they felt for one another translating itself into a blissful surrender to the senses. The wildness that had distinguished their other encounter was tempered by the knowledge that this was not a hasty coupling in a hotel room, but an eager affirmation of their need for one another. This time there would be no regrets, no embarrassment, no desire to escape before recriminations crowded everything else out of her mind. Isobel had never stopped loving Jake. What she was beginning to believe with a sense of wonder was that perhaps he still loved her, too.

She could feel the beat of his heart, its rapid tattoo matching hers. Her hands tugged his tee shirt out of his pants, sliding beneath to spread against the smooth, warm skin of his back, and he shivered.

'I want you,' he said, his teeth against her neck. 'I want you so much. Sometimes I think I've never stopped wanting you.'

Isobel caught her breath. 'I want you, too.' She lifted her face to trail her lips along the roughened line of his jaw. Her voice broke as she added, 'So much.'

Jake made an anguished sound deep in his throat, his hands cupping her bottom to hold her even closer. His mouth found hers again, his tongue plunging hungrily between her teeth to plunder the sweetness within. He was hungry for her, and for a few mindless minutes they were both indifferent to anything but their need of one another. The fact that Mrs Edwards might come to make a start on the breakfast and find them in what she would determine

was a compromising position was submerged beneath emo
tions far too strong to be denied.

Isobel felt her eyes closing, felt Jake's fingers searching
for the snap of her jeans, heard his frustrated curse when
the button refused to give to his efforts. 'Dammit,' he said
a reluctant grin tugging at the corner of his mouth. 'I want
to love you, woman!'

Isobel returned his smile, her love for him shining in her
eyes, and he bent towards her again. 'Do you have any idea
how much I love you?' he breathed huskily, but before she
could answer she saw the sudden movement behind him
The kitchen door was opening, and in the few seconds it
took her to register the fact Emily, still in her pyjamas
slipped into the room.

'Who are you talking to, Daddy?' she asked sleepily
wiping her eyes. Then she saw Isobel sliding out from be
hind her father and her jaw dropped. 'Mummy! Mummy!'
she cried, as soon as she could find her tongue. 'Oh
Mummy, you've come back!'

She covered the floor in a few eager strides, flinging
herself at her mother with an eagerness that nearly knocked
Isobel off her feet. Her legs were already weak from Jake's
lovemaking, and she was glad that the counter was behind
her for added support. Incredibly, Emily seemed to have
grown in her absence, but her bony arms were incredibly
sweet about her waist.

'Hello, baby,' she said, using the affectionate term she
hadn't used for years, and Emily pulled a wry face.

'Where have you been, Mummy?' she exclaimed, draw
ing back to look reprovingly at her. 'I've missed you so
much. We all have—haven't we, Daddy?'

'What? Oh, yeah, right,' Jake's response was ruefully
resigned. He was still standing with his hands braced
against the drainer, and Isobel knew he was finding it

stinct effort to hide his frustration. 'You don't know how
much we've missed you.'

'Oh, I've got some idea,' murmured Isobel teasingly, and
felt so good when Jake pushed himself away from the
nk and came to slip his arm about her shoulders.

'I guess you have at that,' he murmured, just for her, and
en, putting his other arm about his daughter, he drew
em close. 'My two loves,' he said with satisfaction. 'What
y we go out for breakfast? I think this calls for a cele-
ation, don't you, Em? Mummy's back to stay and we're
ll going to be a family from now on.'

Emily gasped. 'Is that true? Mummy, is that true? Is
addy going to live with us from now on?'

'That's what he said,' said Isobel gently, looking at Jake
gain. 'Are you pleased?'

'Of course. Of course I'm pleased!' Emily was ecstatic.
Oh, Mummy, why did you stay away so long?'

'Your mother needed time to forgive me,' said Jake, tak-
g the blame onto his broad shoulders. 'This was never
out you, Em. It was about your mother and me. And, like
lot of good men before me, I got it wrong.'

'But it's all right now?'

'Yeah, it's all right now,' agreed Jake huskily, hugging
obel close to him. 'You'll understand one day. Men can
 awful idiots at times.'

'Like Mr Mallory?'

'Yeah.' Jake pulled a wry face. 'Exactly like Mr Mallory.
ut we put him straight, didn't we, Em? We told him he
asn't welcome here and this time I don't think he'll be
oming back.'

Isobel caught her lower lip between her teeth. 'He—he'd
pset my mother, hadn't he?' she murmured. 'What was
at all about?'

'He didn't like the way you'd treated him,' Jake told her
iefly. 'He was threatening to tell you—well, you know

what he was threatening to tell you. The old lady wasn'
having that.'

'So that's why she told me,' said Isobel, her lips twistin,
a little bitterly. 'I should have known.'

'Don't judge her too harshly, Belle.' Jake could affor
to be generous now. 'She's a sick old woman who's waste
her life and ours trying to hang onto bricks and morta
Deep inside she knew it wasn't worth it, but she'll neve
admit it.'

Isobel sighed. 'I suppose I ought to go up and tell he
I'm back.'

Jake squeezed her shoulder. 'It would be a kindness.'

'Would it?' Isobel grimaced. 'Do you think she cares?

'She cares,' Jake assured her firmly. 'Just don't tell he
I told you so.'

'But where have you been, Mummy?' protested Emily
feeling as if she was being sidelined by the adults. 'Hav
you been staying at a hotel?'

'Mummy can tell us all about it over breakfast,' Jak
said, nodding towards her Winnie the Poohs. 'Why don'
you go and put some clothes on? I don't think McDonald
is equipped to handle a pyjama party.'

'McDonalds! Yippee!' Emily was delighted at the news
and with a final look at her mother, as if to reassure herse
that she was still there, she skipped excitedly out of th
room.

'McDonalds?' murmured Isobel, after she'd gone. 'S
that's how you won her round so completely.'

'Hey, I have my uses,' said Jake modestly. Then h
pulled her close again. 'Don't think I've finished with yo
madam. When we get back from the restaurant I intend t
have suitable compensation.'

'Promises, promises,' whispered Isobel softly. Then, be
fore he could grab her again, she too danced lightly out
his reach.

                    *   *   *

Her mother was awake when she entered the bedroom. Someone—Emily, probably—had drawn back the curtains, and the sun was streaming unrelentingly into the room. It highlighted her mother's face, showed up the lines of pain and fatigue that were etched there. Isobel's heart softened at the realisation that Lady Hannah looked so much worse now than she'd done before.

'Isobel,' she said weakly, as soon as her daughter appeared in the doorway. 'Oh, Isobel, Emily told me you were back, but I could hardly believe it.' She held out a trembling hand towards her. 'Come here, darling. Please. I'm so sorry you felt you had to run away.'

Isobel moved into the room, but she didn't take the old woman's hand. Instead she stood at the end of the bed, trying to decide how she really felt about her mother. There was anger there, and resentment, as well as a sense of incredulity that her mother could have deceived her for so many years.

'How are you?' she asked, deciding it was the least emotive thing she could say, and Lady Hannah's hand fell heedlessly to the coverlet.

'How do I look?' she asked, with a little of her old arrogance. 'I'm as well as can be expected, I suppose. Considering my own daughter walked out on me when I needed her most.'

Isobel shook her head. 'You don't change, do you, Mama? You still think the world owes you its support.'

Lady Hannah's face exhibited its aristocratic detachment for a moment. Then it crumpled, and in a quivering voice she said, 'Is that what you think of me?' She bent her head and plucked at the bedcover. 'I know I did wrong, but I did it because I thought it was best for you.'

'Best for me?' Isobel gasped. 'You knew I didn't care

about Piers Mallory. I loved Jake. But you couldn't stand me making a decision for myself.'

'That's not true.'

'It is true.' Isobel realised she was getting upset herself and reined in her anger. 'Mama, for once in your life admit it: you wanted to control my life.'

'I wanted you to marry someone who had the money to—to care for you.'

'To care for Mattingley, you mean.' Isobel's fingers dug into the wooden footboard of the bed. 'What a useless exercise that turned out to be.'

'I know that now.'

'You knew it then,' Isobel contradicted her coldly. 'You knew it as soon as you learned I was pregnant with Jake's child. But you couldn't admit you'd lied to me, couldn't admit that you'd conspired with Piers to deceive Jake. You preferred to keep us apart so that I wouldn't find out what a pathetic excuse for a mother you'd turned out to be.'

Lady Hannah sighed. 'If you say so.'

'Isn't it the truth?'

'Yes. Yes, all right. I was foolish. But I lost out, too.'

Isobel's brows drew together. 'How?'

'Why do you think the estate has dwindled so inordinately all these years?'

Isobel considered. 'You told me it was because of death duties when Grandpa and my father died.'

'That, too, of course.' Lady Hannah moistened her lips. 'But Piers has had his pound of flesh. He didn't agree to keep his mouth shut for nothing, you know.'

Isobel stared at her. 'He's been blackmailing you?' She was horrified.

'Not that, no.' Lady Hannah's fingers plucked more strenuously at the threads of the coverlet. 'It was the land, you see. The land the Mallorys always wanted. I've sold him parcels of it over the years. For a pittance, of course.

Isobel was appalled. Leaving the end of the bed, she
pproached the old lady slowly. 'So that's why you went
 Jake for money. Because you didn't have enough to keep
e house intact.'

'Something like that,' agreed her mother, looking up at
er anxiously. 'Can you ever forgive me?'

Isobel pressed her lips together. 'I suppose I'm going to
ave to,' she said. 'At least I'm beginning to understand
hat Piers has had over you all these years.'

'Well, he wants it all,' said the old lady wearily. 'And
ter I've gone he'll no doubt get it. I wanted to change
y will and leave the house to Jake, but he won't have any
f it.'

'Do you blame me?'

Isobel glanced towards the door and saw her husband
anding there, a rueful look upon his lean dark face.

'Do you think I want to risk anything else coming be-
ween us?' he asked her huskily. 'But this house can be
urs, Belle. If you want it. I'll make sure the mortgages
e paid off.'

'Oh, Jake…'

Isobel would have gone to him then, needing his strength
ery badly at that moment, but somehow her mother caught
er hand.

'Let him do it,' she begged, as Isobel looked from her
usband to her mother and back again. 'Let him do this for
ou and for Emily. Don't let Piers have his way.'

'Mama—'

'We'll think about it,' said Jake flatly, coming to take
obel's other hand and bestowing a kiss on her knuckles.
f it's what Belle wants…' He shrugged. 'Why don't you
t her decide?'

was snowing.
Isobel stood in the window of their bedroom at

Mattingley, watching the heavy flakes beginning to cove
the trees in the copse. Below her, the terrace was already
coated with white, and she wondered if for once they were
going to have a white Christmas.

'You're going to be frozen,' murmured a deep voice be
hind her, and Isobel smiled as her husband's arms slipped
about her. He drew her back against his warm nakedness
his hands curving possessively over the full swell of her
stomach.

Isobel was already six months pregnant with their second
child, and they'd decided the baby had been conceived in
Jake's room at the pub in the village.

'I was just wondering if we were going to have a white
Christmas,' she said, leaning back against him and loving
the lean power of his body. 'Besides which, your son
doesn't want to go to sleep. He'd been kicking like mad
for the past hour.'

'Yeah, I can feel him,' said Jake, bending his head to
bestow a lingering kiss on the soft skin of her neck. 'Is
there anything I can do?'

'Just hold me,' said Isobel, tipping her head back against
his shoulder. 'It's so peaceful here. We could be alone in
the world. Thank goodness Shane agreed to act as your
deputy.'

'I think two other people would take exception to your
theory,' remarked Jake drily. 'Emily's already talking about
inviting Lucy Daniels to stay. She wants to introduce her
to the friends she's made at her new school. And your
mother seems to have acquired a new lease on life since
she transferred the deeds of the house into your name.'

'I know.' Isobel couldn't help feeling pleased at the re
minder. It was good to know that she and her mother were
reconciled at last, and the new baby would put its own seal
on their relationship 'Do you think the doctors could have
been mistaken in their diagnosis about her?'

'I think she feels she's got something to live for now,' said Jake gently. He massaged his wife's stomach with possessive hands. 'I know I do.'

'Oh, Jake…' Isobel turned towards him then, pressing her fullness against his swelling shaft. 'I do love you.'

'And I love you,' he said tenderly. 'Come back to bed.'

'In a minute.' Isobel cupped his face between her palms and looked at him. 'I want to thank you first. You've done so much for us.'

'Belle—'

'No, I mean it.' She brushed her lips across his protesting mouth. 'Paying off the mortgages on Mattingley, making this a real home again.'

'Sweetheart, it's what I wanted, too.'

'I know. But you didn't have to set up an office here. And you've treated my mother with so much kindness and respect.'

'Hey, she's the only mother I'm ever likely to have,' he assured her gruffly. 'And who else but Lady Hannah plays such a mean game of Predators?'

'That's because she is one,' remarked Isobel drily, and then giggled. 'Besides, I thought you said Emily was your best competition yet.'

'I have to keep all my ladies happy, don't I?' he teased, but his eyes darkened as they rested on her mouth. 'Now, can we go back to bed?'

'Speaking of Predators,' murmured Isobel softly. 'I never did tell you where I thought you got that name from…'

The world's bestselling romance series.

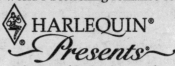

HARLEQUIN®
Presents

Seduction and Passion Guaranteed!

Coming soon...
To the rescue...armed with a ring!

Marriage is their mission!

Look out for more stories of
Modern-Day Knights...

Coming next month:
NATHAN'S CHILD
by Anne McAllister
#2333

Coming in August
**AT THE SPANIARD'S
PLEASURE**
by Jacqueline Baird
#2337

**Pick up a Harlequin
Presents® novel and
you will enter a world
of spine-tingling
passion and provocative,
tantalizing romance!**

Available wherever Harlequin books are sold.

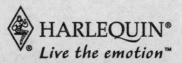

HARLEQUIN®
Live the emotion™

Visit us at www.eHarlequin.com

HPMDNNC

Harlequin Books presents

LEGACIES. LIES. LOVE.

An exciting, new, 12-book continuity launching in August 2003.

Forrester Square...the elegant Seattle neighborhood where the Kinards, the Richardses and the Webbers lived... until one fateful night that tore these families apart.

Now, twenty years later, memories and secrets are about to be revealed as the children of these families are reunited. But one person is out to make sure they never remember....

Forrester Square... Legacies. Lies. Love.

Look for *Forrester Square*, launching in August 2003 with REINVENTING JULIA by Muriel Jensen.

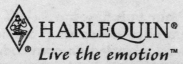

HARLEQUIN®

Live the emotion™

Visit us at www.eHarlequin.com

PHFSG

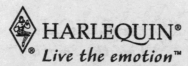

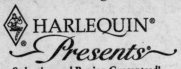

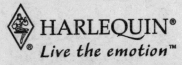